Bounty Hunter

Rye James

Maverick Spur Publishing

Bounty Hunter

Copyright © 2008 by Rye James

This is a work of fiction. All of the characters, names, incidents, and dialogue in this novel are either products of the author's imagination or are used fictitiously.

ISBN: 978-0-615-26404-2

Chapter 1

Riding into town, he knew what kind of looks he'd be getting. It'd be the same looks he got no matter where he went. Being a bounty hunter, he was a friend to no one, and never a welcomed sight. The profession left a bad taste in the mouths of most people. Not that it ever mattered to him what other people thought, as he always was a loner anyway. On this occasion, he was bringing back another victim. Holding the reins of the horse following him with a body draped across its back, he could feel the fingers pointing towards him.

Keeping his eyes focused ahead of him, he rode straight for the sheriff's office. Stopping in front, he stepped down off his Palomino, and walked around to the victim of his Colt. He put his hand on the man's back, and pulled him off the horse, letting the body fall violently to the ground. Brice Symon was a man who law officers were well aware of. If he was on a man's trail, they rest assured that they'd be getting the man's body without a trace of breath left within it. He walked into the sheriff's office, and noticing the lawman at his desk, walked over to him. Symon stood in front of him, pulled out a wanted poster, and dropped it on the desk.

"He's dead, I imagine?" the lawman asked.

"Yep."

"Why do you bounty hunters always bring them in dead? The posters do say dead or alive."

"I'm not the one who made 'em. It gives the option."

"Where's he at?"

"Laying in the dirt out in front."

"Don't have much respect for the dead, do you?"

"I don't hear him complaining."

"Did you give him a chance to give himself up?"

"No, but like I said, I didn't make the poster. He's just as dead with a bullet as he would be at the end of a rope. I just made it quicker."

The sheriff reached into a drawer and pulled out a box. Setting the box on his desk, he opened it to take out the reward money owed to Symon.

"Here's your blood money. Take it and get out of here."

"Don't worry, Sheriff, I don't like being here no more than you enjoy having me. Just one more thing before I go."

Symon reached down to a stack of papers on the sheriff's desk, and began looking through them. He picked out two, folded them, and put them in his shirt pocket.

"Whose death wish do you have in your hands now?"

"Trist Ashton and Sloan Keogh."

"Why them?"

"Gotta be somebody. They're as good as any."

"You sure don't like to make it easy on yourself do you? How long are you staying here?"

"I just want a peaceful hour or two in the saloon, and then I'll be on my way."

"See that you do. I don't want you around here."

Symon walked outside and saw a gathering crowd around the dead body that he left laying on the ground. He looked at them briefly before heading over to the saloon. He went into the saloon, and took to the bar, ordering himself a whiskey. After a few minutes of peacefulness his drinking was interrupted by the town newspaperman.

"You're Brice Symon, are you not?"

Symon turned his head slightly, and glared at him out of the corner of his eye.

"Who wants to know?"

"Well sir, I'm John Nelson, I run the newspaper here in town."

"Go away," Symon said with a soft tone to his voice.

"I was just wondering if I could get a few words from you to do a story."

"A story on what?"

"A story on you. You may well be the most famous bounty hunter in the country. An interview with you would sell a lot of papers."

Symon once again glanced at the reporter, looking at him with contempt. He didn't much care for somebody using him for their own personal gain.

"Beat it," Symon told him again.

Nelson stood there paralyzed, wanting to try and convince Symon to grant him an interview.

"If you don't beat it, somebody else is gonna be doing a story on you...your obituary."

Nelson backed up, and quickly staggered out of the saloon as Symon continued drinking. He was a man of few words, hated small talk, and didn't cotton to most people. He especially liked being left alone, being not too trusting of, or liking strangers. In his late 30's, he'd been a bounty hunter for several years. He wasn't an especially big man, but he could be an intimidating figure when he chose to be. He was left by himself for the next hour, and decided it was time to leave and begin the hunt for his next pair of victims.

He didn't just pick Ashton and Keogh as his next targets out of the blue. He already knew the general direction that they were hanging around. A week or two back he overheard a man who had a little too much to drink talking about the two of them. In his drunken state, he mentioned the area that the pair was in. He apparently was some sort of friend of the duo, or had dealings with them in the past.

Trist Ashton and Sloan Keogh both had $1,000 on their head from the state of Kansas for various robberies, holdups and murder. They usually always traveled together, and sometimes had two or three other men riding along with them. They were rumored to be around Reno at the present time.

As Symon rode along the trail, he kept looking back over his shoulder. Ever since he left town a few days before, he got an undeniable feeling that he was being followed. Although he saw no signs of anyone behind him, he could feel a presence on the back of his heels. Since tracking was his business, his instincts would usually tell him when he was close to someone. And his instincts now were telling him that someone was tailing him.

Whoever it was did not seem to be in any hurry to catch up with him though, so he decided to wait for him. Since night was falling, he made camp with a clump of trees and bushes surrounding him, and built a small fire to make him easy to spot. He put his gear down near the fire and took up position behind some bushes. If the man came in, he'd get the drop on him.

Sure enough, a half hour later, a man approached the camp. As he came in, not noticing anyone around, he took out his gun. He slowly walked towards Symon's saddle and blanket placed near the fire. Symon startled him as he came out of the bushes behind him, pistol in hand.

"Alright, drop the gun," Symon told him.

The stranger let his revolver fall to the ground and slowly turned around to see Symon's gray plated Colt staring at him in the stomach.

"I'm not looking for any trouble," the man stated.

"You've been following me for two days now, what do you want?"

"You're Brice Symon, right?"

"Depends on who's asking."

"My name's Conaghan...Jae Conaghan."

"Don't reckon I know ya."

"I was in town when you brought that man in."

"Keep talking friend."

"Well, I'm assuming you're going after somebody else now."

"You best get to the point fairly quickly here. My finger's getting a little tired."

"I was wondering if I could join up with you."

"Join up with me? Why?"

"I've heard you're one of the best."

"You hear well, but you didn't answer the question. What do you wanna join up with me for?"

"I thought maybe you could teach me how to do things. I'd like to be a bounty hunter too."

"Why?"

"I think I'd be good at it."

Symon looked at him with a certain amount of awe. He could tell the kid had no idea what he was in for.

"How old are you, son?"

"Just turned 19 last month."

Symon began realizing that the kid did not present any danger to him. He shook his head and holstered his pistol. He sat down and started eating some cold beans.

"I don't take apprentices. Besides, I work alone. Sit down and have some grub."

The kid picked up his gun, put it back in his holster, and sat down. Symon tossed him a can of beans. Conaghan looked at Symon, then down at the beans.

"Don't you eat it heated or nothin'?"

Symon couldn't help but be amused by him.

"So hold it over the fire for a few seconds. When you're trailing a man, you don't always get hot meals. Sometimes you can't risk a fire, so you eat it cold. You get used to it after a while."

Symon put the beans aside for a second while looking at the young-ster who was having dinner with him. The kid made him curious.

"What do you want to get started in this line of work for anyway? Ain't you got family or something?"

"No, I've been on my own since I was fourteen when my mother died. I never knew my father. He run out on us before I was even born. I've been working odd jobs around town since then to support myself. I have nothing to keep me there."

"This ain't an easy life, son. You can die awful early if you don't know what you're doing."

"That's why I followed you. You could teach me."

"Ever killed a man before?" Symon asked.

Conaghan stared into the ground, and gently shook his head no.

"Think you could do it if you had to?"

"Yeah."

"What makes you think so?"

"I just know that I can do this."

Symon had serious doubts about the kids' ability to learn the craft, but he definitely seemed eager. At least he had that going for him, if nothing else.

"Do you know what being a bounty hunter means? Or do you just know what the end result is supposed to be."

"Well, I've heard stories."

"I bet you have. I'll tell you how it really is though. You can't have a family cause you're never in one spot long enough to have a home."

"I don't have any kind of family anyway," Conaghan jumped in.

"You have no friends cause you never get close enough to anybody to have any. You're also an outcast in every town you come across who hate what you do. And believe me, there are some who view what we do as worse than the outlaws themselves."

"Well I wasn't exactly enjoying what I was doing back in town any-way."

"You have to be willing to kill anytime, anywhere, in a split second. If you have hesitations, you won't last long. You'll be dealing with danger-ous people who'll have no regrets about putting you six feet under to get you off their trail."

"I understand."

"Think you can handle all that?"

"I'm willing."

"You better be for your sake." Symon took a deep breath, and sighed. "I know I'm gonna regret this, but I'll let you come along for a little while at least."

Conaghan's face lit up with a smile.

"You won't regret it. I'll do whatever you ask."

"Understand one thing though, if you slow me up, or get in my way, I'll leave you in a second."

"Understood," Conaghan replied in agreement. "How'd you get started doing this sort of thing?"

"I more or less stumbled into it a couple years ago. Had no money, no prospects, and no future. Saw a wanted poster of a man, went after him, and found out I was pretty good at this business. Just kept with it after that."

"No family of your own?"

"No. You best turn in soon. We'll get an early start in the morning."

Conaghan went to fetch his stuff, and take care of his horse, so he could bed down for the night. Symon continued sitting by the fire drinking a cup of coffee. His eyes were drawn into the burgeoning flames. Sitting motionless, almost in a trance, he was hypnotized by the fire. Through the ashes he could hear the frightening screams that he'd heard many times before. Unable to look away, he could still hear the woman screaming his name, begging for him to help her. Soon after, he heard a little boy asking him to save him.

They were yelling his name running across a street. He couldn't envision anything other than them running. There were no other people, or buildings. He heard them saying his name right after each other in rapid succession, over and over again. They were the driving force behind him becoming a bounty hunter. Those screams kept the hate inside of him flowing, enabling him to kill without hesitation. It was not always a nightly occurrence, but it happened more frequently than not.

"Brice, you OK?" Conaghan said, breaking Symon's concentration on the fire.

Symon looked up at him without answering, and seemed startled and shaken. Conaghan put his hand on Symon's shoulder, sensing that he was troubled by something. Conaghan's voice broke his attention away from the woman and the little boy. The voices had stopped echoing through his mind, and the visions had now disappeared.

"Brice, what's the trouble?" he asked again, trying to un-shake him.

"It's nothing, kid, don't worry about it. Just was thinking about something for a second."

"Anything you need to talk about?" Conaghan asked with concern.

"No, I'm fine, thanks though. We both better get some sleep. We got a long day ahead of us tomorrow."

Symon was up early in the morning. The sun had barely shown its existence yet. He made some coffee and breakfast then woke up Conaghan.

"Planning on sleeping all day, are ya?" Symon cracked.

Conaghan looked up to the darkness in the skies.

"All day? It's not even light out yet."

Symon handed him a plate of food, and a cup of coffee.

"Careful, it's actually warm," he joked.

"Wonders never cease. Where are we heading for, anyway?" Conaghan wondered.

"Reno."

"What's there?"

"Reckon we'll find out."

"What do you mean?"

Symon reached into his pocket, and pulled out the two wanted posters. He handed them to Conaghan for him to look over.

"These the fellas we're after?"

"Yep."

"They're in Reno?"

"Rumored to be around those parts. Who knows if they're still there though."

"Have you ever come across these men before?"

"Never laid eyes on them."

"How will we know if it's them then?"

"We'll do some asking around town, and dig up some information. Any favorite spots they frequent, things like that. When we come across them, we'll know it."

"What do we do when we find them?"

"We kill them."

"The posters say dead or alive though."

"I only work one way, and that's if they're dead. I don't take prisoners. Dead men have no way to escape, or kill you on the way back. And they'd be desperate enough to try anything."

"How do we split the money?"

"If you do your fair share then we'll each take half."

"How long do you think it'll take us to find them?"

"Depends. A week, a month, a few months...ain't no way of telling for sure."

"If they're only wanted in Kansas, why don't they just leave the state?"

"I reckon cause they're creatures of habit. They'll stay around the same territory, and assume they'll be able to do what they've always done. Most men believe that they're unbeatable, or won't die, so it inflates their ego. They won't do the smart thing, so they'll stick around, and that'll be their downfall. And that's how we'll catch them."

They broke camp and mounted their horses to start on their journey to Reno. Along the way, Conaghan kept firing away at Symon with more questions. He was very eager to learn all he could. Symon didn't mind answering any questions about the profession, but he shied away from anything personal. He basically sidestepped any questions about what he did before he was a bounty hunter. He was beginning to like the kid, though he thought he seemed a little too eager. Although it was something to be expected at Conaghan's age, he just hoped he could hold up when things got rough.

When they arrived in Reno, Symon told Conaghan to put the horses in the stable and meet him in the saloon. He also informed him not to talk to anybody along the way. Within a few minutes, Conaghan had met back up with him in the saloon. Conaghan pulled up a chair and sat down with him at the table.

"Why so secretive?" Conaghan asked.

"People tend to clam up and act differently when they know you're a bounty hunter. Especially if they're friends of the man you're after. They'll talk a little bit more freely if you lie to them."

"That doesn't seem too honorable."

"This isn't an honorable business. If you wanna be honorable, take up preachin'."

"I guess that was a pretty dumb thing to say."

"I'd say," Symon sarcastically remarked as he took a sip of his whiskey.

"So when do we start asking around?"

"Not yet. No need to rush things, we just got here. People might get the wrong idea."

"Who do we ask first?"

"Bartender," Symon said looking to the bar.

"Why him?"

"Every man who passes through a town stops in the saloon. Sometimes information slips out between bottles, or between women. The bartender sometimes knows more things than the sheriff."

After an hour of sitting there, drinking and talking, the two bounty hunters made their way to the end of the bar. Symon called the bartender down for a drink. When he got there, Symon had some questions waiting.

"I hear Trist Ashton's been around these parts lately," Symon said softly, not wanting to be overheard by anyone.

"Yeah, that's what I've heard," the bartender replied with a slight quiver in his voice.

The two locked eyes, and Symon could tell that he knew more than what he said. Symon motioned with his finger for the bartender to come back down, which he did.

"So what do you know about him?" Symon said, still speaking in a low voice.

"Just what I've heard."

"Do you know where he's at?"

"Depends on who's asking."

Symon leaned forward over the bar, getting next to the bartender's ear.

"I am," he said, with a noticeable touch of anger in his voice.

"You a bounty hunter?"

"I'm not gonna ask you twice. If you don't tell me what you know, I'll break every bone in your body. And in case you think that's an idle threat I'm making, you go right ahead and keep playing dumb."

The bartender quickly came to the conclusion to tell the man everything he knew, as he didn't look like a man with a lot of patience. He began washing a few glasses while telling Symon what he wanted to know.

"Right in back of you, there's a man sitting at a table by himself towards the corner. He's been in here before, but I don't know his name. He said once before when he was a little drunk that he occasionally rode with Ashton. He might be able to tell you more. That's all I know, I swear."

Symon put a couple dollars down on the bar for the information.

"Thanks for the tip," Symon said.

"So do we go over there now?" Conaghan asked.

"Not yet. If we did, it might seem like we got the information from the bartender and you never tip off who your sources are. Never know when you might need them again."

Symon took a brief glimpse of the man sitting in the corner, just to get a look at him, and nudged Conaghan in the stomach to follow him. They walked out of the saloon, and Symon told his partner to get them a room at the hotel, while he waited outside the saloon for the man to come out. He found himself a chair beside the saloon window, and leaned back, as he patiently waited. Conaghan returned a few minutes later after securing themselves a room for that night.

"Why are we gonna stay the night? What if he leaves right now?" Conaghan questioned.

"Makes no difference. We're getting the answers we want before he leaves town."

"You mean we're not gonna follow him out of town?"

"Now why would we do that?"

"He could lead us right to Ashton and Keogh."

"He might, then again, he might not. How do you know where he's going? For all we know, we could follow him to his mother's house."

"What makes you think he'll tell us anything?"

"Cause we're gonna threaten him."

"What if that doesn't work with him?"

"It'll work. We'll carry it out till it does."

Chapter 2

After sitting there a few minutes longer, Symon instructed Conaghan to go wait by the hotel. If he wasn't just passing through, then he probably either had a room there, or would be getting one. Conaghan could then follow him into the hotel to see what room he had taken up. A short time later, the man came walking out of the saloon. As Symon suspected, he walked across the street, heading straight for the hotel. The moment the man disappeared into the hotel, Symon started walking to it.

Symon met up with Conaghan inside the hotel, and Conaghan let him know the man went up to the second floor, though he didn't see what room. They went up to the man behind the check-in desk to see if they could figure it out.

"Can I help you sir?" the man asked.

"Sure hope so. I was wondering what room number the man who just came in here had. He looked like an old friend of mine who I haven't seen in some years. I'd like to go up and say hello to him," Symon responded.

"Oh, Mr. Williams, you mean?"

"Yes, that's him. Good ol' Willy," Symon said with a chuckle.

"Sure, he's in room 14 on the second floor."

"Room 14...got it. I sure do appreciate your help, thank you kindly."

Symon and Conaghan proceeded to go upstairs to the second floor to find Williams' room.

"Ever hear of this Williams before?" Conaghan asked.

"Doesn't seem to ring a bell, but don't let him know it when we get in there."

They found room 14, and figured out the easiest and safest way to talk to him. Symon stood close to the wall next to the door, out of the line of sight. Conaghan knocked on the door, and Williams slightly opened it, just enough to see who it was. The moment Williams asked what Conaghan wanted Symon's fist jumped out, and delivered a devastating punch to Williams' jaw, knocking him completely on his back.

They rushed into the room with their pistols drawn. Williams started to draw his gun while he was on his back, but upon seeing two guns pointing at him, thought better of it. Conaghan reached down and took the gun out of Willams' holster, unloaded the bullets, and gave it back to him. Symon motioned for Willams to take a seat on the bed, which he complied with.

"What do you guys want with me?" Willams worried.

"Information, Willy, information," Symon mused.

"What kind of information?"

"I want to know where Ashton and Keogh are."

"Who?"

"Don't get cute, Williams. They're the most well known outlaws in Kansas, you know exactly who they are."

"How do you know my name, anyway?"

"It's my job to know things like that."

"Bounty hunters?"

Symon answered him with a grin.

"Now where are they?" Symon asked.

"What makes you think I know?"

"You've ridden with them before, so I'm guessing you know exactly where they are."

"I don't know where they're at."

Symon took a deep sigh, signaling his unhappiness to Williams.

"I'm not a patient man, Willy. You've got about five minutes to tell us what you know," Symon said angrily.

As Williams was trying to mull over his options, Symon gave him something else to think about. He pulled a folded wanted poster out of his shirt pocket, and held it up.

"Know what this is?"

Williams had a good idea of what Symon was holding, and the thought of it held back his words to respond.

"You're worth $500, Williams, dead or alive."

"I ain't done nothin' to deserve that."

"Oh, but you have. Seems as though everyone knows who you've been riding with. Says on here you're wanted for robbery. Now it seems to me that we got two options here. Wanna know what they are?"

"Keep talking."

"I'm Brice Symon. Ever heard the name before?"

"Yeah, I've heard of ya. You're just as bad as any outlaw. Every person you bring in rides a horse the same way...on his belly. Don't even give a guy a chance."

"Well that's not true, Willy. I'm giving you the same chance that you'd give me...none. But I like you, Willy, so here's what I'll do for you. You tell me where Ashton and Keogh are, and I'll forget that I saw you. You can go anywhere you want, I won't tell anyone where you are, and I won't be coming for you."

"They'd kill me if they knew I sent you after them," Williams worriedly said.

"Not if I kill them first," Symon said bluntly. "You know my reputation. You got as much reason to fear me as them. You've got to consider the consequences if you don't tell me what I want to know."

"I'm unarmed. You got no call to kill me now."

Symon took Willams' gun, then walked over to Conaghan and took one of the bullets out of his hand. He placed one bullet in the gun, and spun the chamber. He then tossed the gun back to Williams and told him to stand up.

"What's this?" Williams wondered.

"I'm giving you your chance. If that bullet's in the firing chamber, and you kill me, you get to walk out of here. Jae here will let you be. If you're not so lucky, then we get $500, and my reputation is left intact."

"What kind of odds is that?"

"Not very good ones. But I'm giving you a choice, your life for theirs. I want them, but you'll due if that's how you choose it to be."

It didn't take Williams very long to decide on an answer. Only a few seconds later he threw the gun down to the floor. He knew the odds were stacked against him, and he didn't consider Ashton and Keogh close enough friends to take that risk.

"Alright, you win," Williams muttered. "I don't know exactly where they are, but I know how you can find out."

"I'm listening."

"There's a woman whose name is Mary Ford. She always knows where Ashton is, or where he's going, or what he's done."

"What's she to him, his girl?"

"Yeah, and you'll do yourself a favor by being careful around her. She's a feisty one, and she ain't above shooting a man to protect Ashton either."

"And where's she at?"

"She lives in Kingman. She does some singing in the saloon there."

"Does everybody know she's Ashton's girl?"

"Yeah. Ashton goes in there a lot."

"Why doesn't the sheriff arrest him?"

"As long as Ashton doesn't cause any trouble while he's in town, he lets him be. As long as things are kept peaceful in town, he doesn't care who you are."

"What about Keogh?"

"He's usually with him. They never stay separated for too long. Where you find one the other's not too far behind."

"Thanks for the information. I'll give you a little advice before I go, don't go hanging around Ashton and Keogh in the coming weeks, it wouldn't do much for your health."

"Don't worry I'm not planning on it."

Conaghan dropped the rest of the bullets he was holding on the floor, and he and Symon left Willams' room. As they were walking back down the stairs, Conaghan was asking about some of the things Williams told them.

"You believe everything he said?"

"Yeah."

"How do you know he's not just making things up?"

"When the end of your life is staring you in the face, it's not a good time to lie."

"Would you have really killed him?"

"I gave him a bullet, didn't I?"

"Whose wanted poster was it that you showed?"

"Ashton's, but he didn't know that."

"If he knew that it wasn't his, he probably wouldn't have been so open to talk."

"Maybe, but he wasn't in much of a position to bargain. Besides, if he's been riding with them, I'm sure he's wanted somewhere. As an outlaw, you save your own skin first."

"Now we go see Mary Ford?"

"Yeah, we'll start in the morning."

They took up the night in their rooms, and got themselves a good night's sleep. It'd take a couple days before they reached the town of Kingman.

When morning came, the bounty hunters met up with each other in the horse stable. They exchanged pleasantries and got on their way. With them seemingly being very close to the outlaws, they wasted no time in getting to Kingman. They moved swiftly, and reached the town in less than two days, just after sundown. Riding through the street, Symon noticed a lawman watching them from in front of the jail. He'd have to make sure not to cause any suspicions. The law always got jumpy when they knew a bounty hunter was in town.

They dismounted their horses in front the saloon, and went inside. Once inside, they noticed it wasn't just a saloon. It had a stage, most likely for singing and dancing, and some gambling tables. It looked like the place got a lot of action.

Symon and Conaghan walked up to the end of the bar, and waited for the bartender to come down to them.

"So what can I get for you two gentlemen?" the bartender asked.

"You can tell us where Mary Ford is," Symon replied.

"What do you want to know for?"

"Just tell her Ashton sent us."

The bartender stood there looking the two of them over for a minute.

"Wait here," he said, as he walked from out of the bar.

They watched him as he walked through a side door. A few seconds later, he emerged. He let Symon know that she would be out to see them in a second. They eagerly anticipated her coming out. A few seconds later they noticed that side door opening. Out stepped a woman who they assumed had to be Mary Ford. She was very attractive, with a nice figure, and long blonde hair. Symon remembered what Williams told them about her though, so he knew enough to be careful around her.

"You boys have a message for me?" she asked, approaching them.

"Sure do."

"Well what is it?"

"I'd rather not say here," Symon said while he looked around the room.

Ford shook her head in agreement, and told the boys to follow her to her dressing room.

"OK, so what's the message?"

Symon coyly smiled, while hoping she didn't have a gun hidden somewhere in that dress of hers. Cause after what he was about to say, he believed she would use it if she could.

"Well, to be honest, there ain't no message."

A concerned look crept over Ford's face. She sat down while waiting for them to say what they wanted.

"What do you want?" she finally asked.

"Just lookin' for some information, that's all. Then we'll be out of here."

"What kind of information?"

"We want to know where Ashton's at."

"So which are you...lawmen or bounty hunters?"

"You don't see a badge, do you?"

"So you're after Trist Ashton now?"

"And his partner."

"I don't know where they're at."

"You know every move he makes, don't insult us."

"Why are you after him? What's he ever done to you?"

"There's $1,000 on him, that's why I'm after him."

"And you hunt and kill men for money?"

"That's right."

"It doesn't seem to bother you in the least."

"It don't."

"And why is that?"

"They deserve what they got coming."

"And what do you think you have coming?"

"Maybe the same thing."

"The bible says you shouldn't kill."

"It also says an eye for an eye. Strange to hear you talk about that considering who you run around with."

"That doesn't mean I agree with killing."

"No, I reckon not."

"So why do you do it?"

"Somebody's got to."

"I find your profession morally unacceptable and disgusting. What do you think of that?"

"I don't recall asking for your opinion, and I don't think you're one to be talking about morals."

Angry about what he was implying, Ford slapped Symon across the face. Symon slapped her right back, only a little bit harder.

"You're a hard man," she told him as she rubbed her face.

"Been called worse than that. You have to be a hard man to stay alive in this profession."

"Don't you find what you do hypocritical?"

"Look, lady, the whole world is hypocritical. You, me, and everyone in it. The law says you don't kill unless it's in self defense, but how far can you take it? Is it someone who physically comes after you, or is it defending yourself or others from the likelihood of someone doing something before they get the chance to do it."

Ford looks at him quizzically.

"Don't understand me, do you? I protect others by killing outlaws, before they get the chance to kill or rob them."

"I still find it wrong. You're no better than they are."

"Who said I was better? Who's to say what's right and wrong? You do what you want to do, and you put a reason behind it to make it just, fair, or the right thing to do. An outlaw can say he was driven to stealing or killing by getting a raw deal, or saying the deck was stacked against him. I can say I was driven to hunting them cause it pays well, and it's within the law. So who the hell knows what's right."

"How many men have you brought in? 20, 50, 100?"

"Your guess is as good as mine. I don't keep count."

"And how many of those have you brought in dead?"

"All of them."

"So what makes you think that I'd tell you anything about where he is?"

"I don't, you already have."

She looks at him puzzled as to how she could have told him where Ashton was. How could he possibly know when she avoided it during the whole conversation. Symon simply smiled at her, knowing she was confused by what he said. The bounty hunters then excused themselves, walking back to the saloon. Conaghan was just as confused as Ford was.

"What good was all that, she didn't tell us a damn thing," Conaghan wondered.

"It's not what she told us, it's what she'll show us."

"What's that?"

"She'll lead us right to him. Maybe Keogh too if they're riding together right now."

"She'll never lead us to him."

"Not purposely, but she will lead us to him."

"How you figure?"

"If he's in the area, within the next day or so, she'll ride to wherever he is and tell him a couple bounty hunters are close by looking for him. When she does that, we'll follow her out there. We'll ride out of town first though, so she doesn't think we're on her tail."

"You make it sound so simple."

"It is. Things are only as hard as you make them. Everybody has a downfall, and a woman will always be a man's downfall."

"How do you know she'll actually do that?"

"Cause she's concerned about him, and doesn't want him to die. You can tell she's emotionally attached to him. Probably loves him too."

"I guess love kills."

"It will in this case."

"It's too bad it'll end up that way."

"Don't let yourself get personally involved, Jae. It's just a job, nothing more, nothing less. We're not here to side with anybody, or make social statements. We don't make the posters, and we don't make them wanted men. They do that to themselves. If you don't do it, someone else will. You can't let yourself care. If you do, then that'll be your downfall."

"Guess I have a lot to learn."

"You do. It'll come though. You'll get there if you want it bad enough."

"Do you ever wish you were something else? Not a bounty hunter, I mean?"

"I wish a lot of things, boy. Don't make any of them so though."

"Would you change if you could?"

"You have to accept who you are. I've accepted who, and what I am."

The two bounty hunters left the saloon and led their horses across the street to the barber shop. They just stood there leaning against some posts waiting for Mary Ford to come out. It'd prove to be a long wait. After a couple hours there was still no sign of Ford. Conaghan was starting to get a little anxious.

"How much longer we gonna wait here?" the youngster asked.

"Till she comes out," the veteran replied.

Conaghan sighed and tilted his head back looking up at the sky realizing that it'd be a long night.

"Isn't there a better spot we can wait or something?"

"Like where?" Symon asked.

"I dunno. Isn't there something else we could be doing that'd be more productive?"

"Such as?"

"Dunno. Just asking."

After another long hour of anxiously waiting they saw someone walking a saddled horse up to the saloon. Symon figured something was about to happen. Ford finally emerged from the saloon and mounted the horse. She looked around and started to ride out of town at a trot. Conaghan eagerly started for his horse before Symon grabbed his arm.

"Just wait a few minutes," Symon told him.

"Why? She'll be gone by then."

"Not hardly. She's not exactly riding like her hair's on fire. Besides, you don't want her to know we're following her."

About ten minutes later the two bounty hunters mounted their horses and slowly made their way out of town. They just barely saw the outline of a woman disappearing over a hill. They continued their ride towards the woman when Symon started looking back.

"Forget something?" Conaghan asked.

"Not likely."

As they continued riding Symon started staring towards the ground like he was in deep thought. Conaghan noticed Symon seemed to be in a different place.

"See something?"

"Nope," Symon bluntly replied.

"Hear something?"

"Nope."

"Anything?"

"Feel something."

"Huh?" Conaghan asked.

"Feels like we're being followed."

"How can you tell?"

"Can't. Like I said, just a feeling."

"How often do you get these feelings?"

"Sometimes."

"How often are you usually right about them?"

"Mostly."

"Who'd be following us?" Conaghan wondered.

"If I were a betting man, I'd say Ms. Ford up there arranged it."

"She knew we'd be watching where she went," Conaghan stated.

"How long till we reach Ashton and Keogh you think?" Conaghan wondered.

"Don't rightly know. Probably not too long. Day or so."

The two men came across a stream and Symon dismounted to check the ground for fresh hoof prints. The ground would be wet from going through the water. After finding the marks he walked back to his horse and picked up the reins that were hanging down. He mounted and turned his horse to the side and stared out into the dark. He knew someone was coming. He squinted his eyes to try and see any type of movement. He couldn't see anything but blackness though.

"Still think someone's following?" Conaghan asked.

"No doubt about it."

After traveling for another hour they decided to make camp for the night. They noticed a large clump of bushes and trees to bed down. After tying up their horses, they built a fire, then laid down their saddles and blankets to turn in for the night. A few minutes later Symon noticed that Conaghan had fallen asleep already. He quickly got up and grabbed his Colt. He positioned his hat on his saddle and made up his blanket to make it look like he was still laying there. He looked around and slowly walked around one of the thick bushes behind him. Symon deliberately slowed up on the trail to let whoever was behind them time enough to catch up to them. He also built up the fire high enough so that they wouldn't be missed. It didn't take very long. In what seemed like no time at all, Symon could hear the footsteps of men coming closer to their camp. One of them stepped on a small branch making a crackling sound. Symon peered around the edge of the bush he was behind and saw three men approaching the camp with their rifles drawn. One of the men stopped in front of Conaghan while the other two walked over to where Symon's gear was. The men nodded to each other signifying they were all ready and raised their firearms. As soon as they did this, Symon jumped from around the bushes ready to fire.

"Looking for me?" he asked, his finger ready to pull the trigger.

As soon as the men turned to fire, Symon fired multiple shots towards the two men directly in front of him. He hit his first target in the chest and the second in the left shoulder. He fell to the ground to avoid the aim of the third attacker when Conaghan bounced up, grabbed his gun, and shot the man twice in the stomach making him fall into the fire. Symon then fired two more rounds into the man he hit in the shoulder, this time the bullets lodging into the pit of his stomach. Smoke filled the air. Symon then propped himself up to his knees, looked around, and breathed a big sigh of relief. All three of the men following them were dead. Symon got to his feet and looked over the two men on the ground to make sure they were dead. He then walked over to the man who had fallen into the midst of the fire and kicked him off of it. He looked over to Conaghan to make sure he was OK.

"You alright?"

"Yeah," he replied back, looking around at the dead bodies. He wasn't quite sure what to do or say. He wasn't sure how he was supposed to feel after killing a man.

"Know any of 'em?" Conaghan asked.

"Can't say that I do," Symon replied.

He looked back to Symon and saw him laying back down again.

"What are you doing?" Conaghan asked.

"Going to bed," Symon said, looking back at him.

"How can you sleep after this?" Conaghan asked in amazement.

"Easy. I'm tired. So should you."

"Even with them laying there?"

"Why, does it bother you?"

"Just a little."

"Then move them," Symon told him.

Symon then turned over and went to sleep much to Conaghan's astonishment. He couldn't believe how he could just go to sleep after killing two men without it seeming to bother him even a little bit. He wondered if eventually he'd get like that. Conaghan definitely knew he couldn't go back to sleep after all that, and grabbed a shovel. Even though the men had just tried to kill them he figured they at least deserved to be buried. Upon awaking in the morning, Symon noticed the three freshly dug graves, and wandered over to them. After looking them over for a few minutes he walked back over to where Conaghan was standing.

"Mighty nice of you to bury them fellas," Symon noted.

"Someone had to."

"Not really."

"You would've just left them out in the open?" Conaghan asked.

"Animals gotta eat too," Symon replied.

Chapter 3

They broke camp and immediately picked up Ford's trail. She either didn't know how to hide her tracks or simply didn't care enough to try and lose them. Or maybe she was figuring on them being dead already. The bounty hunters picked up their pace to reach her more quickly. A few hours had passed before Conaghan started getting impatient.

"Shouldn't we have caught this girl by now?"

"You're mighty impatient, aren't ya?" Symon noted.

"Just wanna get this over with."

"Remember, time is your friend. You got all the time in the world to finish the job. Never rush. Rushing is what gets men killed."

"How much longer you figure?"

"Not long. I reckon within an hour or two. Stay alert. If they know we're coming they may have a little surprise for us somewhere along the way."

"Like what?"

"I don't know. That's why I said to stay alert."

They were starting to come across a more rocky terrain that was a little more difficult to ride through. There were a few boulders along with a bunch of trees and bushes, but mostly it was little rocks that were making it an uncomfortable ride. Symon figured that it was probably by design. He pulled up on the reins of his horse and dismounted with Conaghan following him.

"What's going on?" Conaghan wondered.

"We'll walk the rest of the way."

"Why?"

"I think if we keep on riding we'll wind up with a face full of dirt."

"That close?"

"Reckon so."

The two men started walking with their rifles drawn, being careful as to not make much noise not knowing how close their targets were. Symon figured they'd come across them at any moment. Symon suddenly stopped as he noticed a small cabin in the distance. They tried to make their way up to it without being seen by trying to hide behind the trees and boulders although Symon assumed they knew they were coming. They got within 20 yards when a shot rang out splitting one of the trees they were standing by.

"Well, they know we're here now," Symon stated.

"What do we do?" Conaghan asked.

"Wait for their next move. We don't have to go anywhere. It's up to them."

Symon instructed Conaghan to try and make his way around to the side of the cabin to try and get a better look.

"How do I know which one Ashton or Keogh is?" Conaghan asked.

"Don't matter."

"How's that?"

"Just shoot whoever is in your way."

Symon maneuvered behind a rock which provided pretty good cover.

"How long you figurin' on waitin' in there?" Symon shouted to the cabin.

"As long as it takes," someone shouted back.

"You gotta come out sometime."

"You're assuming we're stuck here."

"Seems like you are."

"You're under the impression that nobody's coming up behind ya."

Symon quickly turned his head back. He didn't figure that maybe they were being trapped. Although it occurred to him that they might be bluffing, he stared back at the trees and rocks, his head not moving an inch, his eyes darting side to side looking for any type of movement. He saw nothing though.

"You're under the impression that I don't got anybody watching back there," Symon responded.

Symon took the chance that they were bluffing and called them on it figuring it might speed up things. They exchanged a few rounds neither doing much but filling the air with smoke. A few minutes later the outlaws made a break for it. Three men and a woman burst out of the front door, guns blazing, trying to make it around to the back of the cabin. Symon returned fire with his rifle hitting one man in the leg, and another in the stomach causing both men to fall on the ground moaning in pain. One man and the woman made it around the cabin where he hoped Conaghan was able to get them. Symon stepped in front of the boulder to get a better shot at the men on the ground who were still able to put up a fight. He lodged a second shot, this time fatal, into the one man's stomach as he was rising up with a pistol in his hand. He then set sights on the man with the wounded leg, hitting him with a shot to the chest as he was reaching for his revolver. He heard another shot ring out from around back which he hoped was Conaghan. He quickly ran around back to see Ashton and Ford standing with their hands in the air with Conaghan holding a gun on them.

"What's this?" Symon asked with a tint of anger in his voice.

"They were running toward their horses and I fired a shot at their feet to let them know I had 'em," Conaghan explained.

"We don't give no warning shots here!"

"Much obliged to you, son," Ashton told Conaghan.

"Shut up!" Symon yelled, looking back at Ashton.

"They gave themselves up," Conaghan tried to tell him.

"You had a clear shot."

"In the back?"

"A clear shot's a clear shot."

"Backshooter. Seems to me that's just as bad as the men you hunt," Ford interrupted.

"Listen lady, when you're dealing with scum it don't matter how you bring them in, as long as it's one way…dead."

"So what are you going to do now, Mr. Symon, shoot us both?" Ford asked.

Symon took a big sigh not liking the situation one bit.

"What about the other boys, they dead?" Ashton asked.

"You don't see anyone else moving, do you?" Symon responded.

"Should I get them?" Conaghan asked.

"No, not with these two still breathing. We'll have a tough enough time just bringing them in."

Symon motioned for Conaghan to tie their prisoners' hands together.

"Alright, here's the deal. I'll take you in alive, but the first time you try something, I'll kill you as sure as you're standing there, and you know I'll do it."

"I'm not the one you have to worry about," Ashton pointed out.

"Is that so?"

"You know as well as I do Sloan's not too far away. How far you think you're gonna get?" Ashton said with a devilish grin.

"We'll see. I might not make it, but you sure won't either."

They walked down the path to where Symon and Conaghan's horses were before starting on their way back to Kingston.

"Just so you know, them other boys met their makers too," Symon told Ford.

"You killed them too?" Ford asked.

"Already said as much, repeating it won't make it any different."

"How does one get to be as hard a man as you?" she wondered.

"You lose everything in your life that's important," he replied.

Ashton rode in front with Ford behind him then Conaghan and Symon riding behind her.

"Guess I messed things up, huh?" Conaghan asked.

"We'll see. Hope it won't wind up killing the both of us."

"Think Keogh's coming like he said?"

"Yep. Only question is whether he can get to us before we get to town. And you can bet Ashton's gonna try and slow us up to buy him time. That's why you don't take prisoners. You wind up putting yourself in a jam."

"I'll make it up to you."

"Hopefully you won't have to."

Ashton kept looking to his left like he was waiting for Keogh to come galloping along any minute. Symon noticed and started looking to both sides and behind him. He could feel that Keogh was near.

"Hey Symon! Mind if we stop for some water?" Ashton asked.

"Keep riding," Symon replied bluntly.

"What, are you gonna let me die of thirst?"

"It occurred to me."

Ashton deliberately tried slowing his horse up to buy him some time. After a few hours of riding, the prisoners were starting to wonder when they were gonna break for camp.

"Are we making camp soon, Mr. Symon?" Ford asked.

"Not yet."

"How much farther do you plan on riding?"

"A little further."

"I don't know how much further I can go without a break."

"You'll go as far as I tell ya."

"You don't have an ounce of decency for anybody do you?"

"Not for the likes of you two."

"Maybe I've decided I'm not going any farther."

"Then you can get off your horse and I'll leave you here."

"Looks like he got you on that one, Mary," Ashton chimed in laughing.

"I wouldn't be so happy if I was you," Symon told him.

"Why not? I have as good a chance of hanging as you do."

"Could be, but you also have as good a chance of being shot, so think of that."

"You're pretty sure of yourself," Ashton said.

"About as much as you are I suppose."

"I guess that's why you're as good as you are, huh?"

"I guess."

"You're not much for talking, are ya?"

"Not much," Symon bluntly stated.

"I tell ya what, I'll make a deal with you."

"Not interested."

"No, hear me out first. You know Keogh's out there, right?"

"Maybe."

"Ain't no maybe, my friend, that's a guarantee. Let us go and I give you my word no harm will come to ya."

"And how much is that worth?"

"I may have done a lot of stuff, but a man's got to have his word."

"I'll give it some thought."

"That's all I can ask."

They continued riding till nightfall before making camp.

"I hope you're not thinking of asking me to make dinner because I assure you I will not," Ford told Symon.

"Wouldn't dream of asking you."

"So what do you plan on us eating?"

Symon went for his saddle bags and pulled out a few cans of beans which he tossed to everybody.

"Aren't you gonna make a fire?" she asked.

"No," he replied with a shake of his head.

"You want us to eat them cold?"

"If I can do it, so can you."

After they finished eating, Ford was wondering about the sleeping arrangements.

"I suppose you'll tie us up while we're sleeping too," she sarcastically said.

"As a matter of fact, I am."

"I can't sleep with my hands tied."

"Then it looks like you're not sleeping tonight."

Symon then sat Ashton and Ford with their backs to a tree and tied their hands behind them. He wasn't taking any chances of them doing something during the night to cause trouble.

"You're a careful man," Ashton said.

"Reckon I am."

Symon told Conaghan that they'd sleep in shifts so one of them could keep an eye out if Keogh were to show up, or Ashton and Ford started any trouble. Symon decided he'd take the first shift. He propped himself up against a tree across from his prisoners with his rifle across his lap as Conaghan bed himself down for a few hours.

"Given my offer any more thought?" Ashton asked.

"No deal."

"You're a stubborn man, Symon. Gets too many a men killed."

"Can't argue with that."

"So why not save yourself?"

"Maybe I like the challenge."

"Well if you're looking to exit this world hastily, just untie me, give me your gun and I'll do the honors for ya."

Symon smiled and chuckled.

"I've heard of ya before," Ashton told him.

"I'm flattered."

"No, I'm talking serious here. I been hearing stories about you for some time now."

"Nothing too exciting I'm sure."

"Always figured you'd wind up on my tail eventually, just didn't think it'd be so soon."

"No time like the present."

"What got you into this line of work?"

"Just happened into it."

Ashton laughed and could tell Symon was trying to hide something.

"Nobody just happens into anything. You got your reasons but I reckon they're your business."

"They are," Symon answered.

"Looks like it's a little sore spot with you."

"Nope."

Ashton noticed that Symon was tensing up a little with the questions and thought maybe he could get him a little unnerved or find something from his words that he could use at a later time.

"No, I think I did. Not too proud of your past? Done something you're ashamed of?"

"Right now the only thing I'm ashamed of is that I didn't kill you earlier."

"You have a lot of hatred built up inside you."

"Could be."

"So what happened? Someone kill your momma? Someone shoot your dog?"

"You got a big mouth."

"I know it."

"Why are you trying to rile him, Trist?" Ford asked.

"Just havin' some fun with him is all. So what was it, Symon?"

"Shut up," Symon answered softly with a firmness that suggested Ashton should heed his suggestion.

"What, gonna shoot me? Nah, you can't do that. Not unless I tried to escape or somethin'. Shoot a little boy?"

"I'm not gonna tell you again," Symon said looking directly at Ashton with deadly eyes.

"No sense of humor, huh? Have problems with your wife? She left ya for some outlaw? Yeah, that's it, isn't it?"

Symon jumped to his feet and walked over to Ashton standing over him firmly gripping his rifle. Ashton started smiling, realizing that he found something that pushed Symon's buttons.

"Looks like I riled you up some, don't it?"

"Last time, shut your hole."

"OK. OK. Didn't realize you'd be so sensitive about your wife running off on ya. She take your kid too?"

Symon wasn't going to hear any more of his drivel. As soon as the last word left his mouth, Symon took the butt end of his rifle and swung it at Ashton's face hitting him in the left side of his face, knocking his hat off and bruising his jaw and cheekbone.

"Got anything else to say?" Symon angrily asked.

He didn't get an answer as Ashton slumped to his right only being held up by the tree to which he was tied.

"Was that really necessary?" Ford asked.

"Reckon it was."

Symon finished off the rest of his shift without hearing a peep out of Ashton. Ford had fallen asleep and Ashton woke up every now and then with the pain in his face causing him some discomfort. Symon walked over and nudged Conaghan with his boot waking him up to relieve him. Conaghan slowly rose to his feet rubbing the sleep out of his eyes.

"Think he's out there?" Conaghan asked.

"Oh, he's out there. Just a question of where."

"Think he'll try something tonight?"

"Depends how close he is. Just keep your eyes open and stay alert. If Ashton wakes up and starts talking, don't listen to him. He'll say anything to get you to make a mistake."

"No problem."

Conaghan poured himself a cup of coffee before grabbing his rifle to stand watch. It seemed to be a pretty quiet night. It was a clear night, well lit with the moon out. Symon picked a spot near a clump of trees to avoid being out in the open. As the night wore on Conaghan started getting a little jumpy hearing sounds of animals. He heard some birds chirping, rabbits running into bushes, squirrels running up trees, always wondering if something or someone was causing them to stir. Ashton woke up and noticed that Conaghan was getting jittery.

"You alright, boy?"

"I'm fine."

"A little scary knowing someone's out there waiting for you, ain't it?"

"Not really."

"You ain't foolin' me. I can see it. Starting to get a little nervous. He might be watching you right now. Just waiting for you to turn the wrong direction giving him a clear line of fire."

Conaghan turned his head in every direction squinting his eyes to see if he could make out an outline of someone. Ashton was getting to him. Conaghan noticed that he was staring out to his right which made Conaghan nervous.

"What're you looking at?"

"Nothing," Ashton answered, knowing that his plan seemed to be working.

He kept looking out in that direction hoping to make Conaghan think that someone was there. Conaghan snapped his head back in that direction, starting to believe that someone was there.

"Let me go now, and I give you my word that no harm will come to ya," Ashton said, trying to convince him into a release.

"Can't do that."

"Why not?"

"Gave Brice my word."

"Your word's no good to a dead man."

"He's the only man who's ever given me a chance to do something besides cleaning up stables."

"I can understand that. I really can. I can appreciate your respect for the man. How 'bout if I give you my word we'll let him go too."

Conaghan looked over at Symon sleeping and thought back to what he told him about Ashton.

"Brice told me you'd try something like this."

"Like what? Ain't nothin' to try with Keogh out there waiting for you. All I'm trying to do is save your hide, boy. You're as good as dead as soon as we get moving."

"I trust Brice."

"Trust ain't got nothin' to do with dyin'. Lot of good men trusted someone into an early grave. Tell you what, just untie me, I'll go find Sloan and you'll never see us again. Everbody wins."

Conaghan stared at the trees thinking about what he should do. He knew that if Keogh was out there waiting that there was a good chance they'd be killed. But he also knew that Symon had a lot more experience at his profession and trusted he knew what he was doing.

"What do you say?" Ashton asked.

"I think you should go back to sleep."

"You're making a bad mistake."

"I guess we'll find out."

"Can't guarantee you a decent burial."

A few more hours passed with Conaghan anxiously waiting for the sun to come up. Things would seem somewhat safer once the sun came up and he could actually see. The night seemed to play on his mind too much. Symon started moving around a little bit, his eyes slightly opening. He sat up and looked over to make sure everyone was still around. Conaghan was drinking coffee while Ford and Ashton were still sleeping. Symon yawned before stumbling over to grab some coffee too.

"Quiet night?" Symon wondered.

"I heard a lot of noises."

"What kind of noises?"

"Animals and such."

"He move at all?" Symon asked of Ashton.

"Looked out over there for a spell. Thought maybe Keogh was out there."

"He was just trying to spook you."

"Worked for a little bit."

"Nighttime has a tendency to do that. Darkness has a way of making a man see and hear things that ain't really there."

"Well, I reckon we should get them up and moving so we can get out of here. Should I break out some grub?"

"Nah. The sooner we get moving and get to town the better off we'll be. Get the horses ready and I'll get these two moving."

Symon walked over to Ford and Ashton and cut the rope that bound their hands together. The sudden movement woke the pair up.

"Get to your feet. We'll be moving out soon," Symon informed the duo.

They stood up just as a sliver of the morning sun started shining down.

"What's for breakfast?" Ford asked.

"Who said we're eating?"

"Planning on starving us to death?"

"Crossed my mind."

"Why don't you just shoot us and get it over with?"

"Don't tempt me, lady."

"How 'bout some coffee?" Ashton wondered.

"No, I'm good," Symon countered.

"Have you not a decent bone in your body?" Ford angrily asked.

"The sooner we get to town and you two are out of my hair, I'll show you all the decency you can handle."

Conaghan brought the horses up and the four of them mounted after Symon tied Ashton's hands together.

"Still don't trust me, huh?"

Symon just laughed at the question. They were about a half day's ride away from Kingman. Ashton took the lead position with Conaghan, Ford, and Symon following in single file. As they rode along Ashton decided he needed to slow it up a bit to try and give Keogh more time. He deliberately fell off his horse while trying to make it look like he wasn't able to hold on with his hands tied. Symon brought his horse up to where Ashton was now sitting.

"Get on your feet," Symon told him, leaning on the horn of his saddle.

"How am I supposed to stay on my horse?"

"Maybe you should try hanging on with that big mouth of yours."

"If you untie my hands I won't fall off again."

"Get up."

Symon waited for Ashton to stand up before quickly dismounting his horse. In one motion he turned around quickly and landed a punch square on Ashton's face dropping him to the dirt.

"Pull a stunt like that again and I'll hogtie ya."

"Mr. Symon…" Ford started to say before Symon interrupted her.

"I'm through playing games."

They rode along at a pretty good pace for another hour or so before Ashton tried another of his tricks. They were riding along a river when Ashton pulled up on the mare he was riding.

Symon knew he was up to something again.

"What are you stopping for?" Symon yelled.

"I need some water."

Symon spurred his horse on to get next to Ashton.

"So you need some water?"

"Yeah."

Symon let his right hand off his reins and reared back and delivered another blow to Ashton sending him off his horse and into the river.

"Now you got your water," Symon noted.

Ashton stood up on the edge of the river trying to shake some of the wetness off him.

"You hit me for the last time, Symon."

"You're right about that."

"Ain't gonna take it no more."

"You're right again, cause I'm through playing your games."

"Soon as Keogh gets here I'm gonna make sure I kill you myself."

"Well between then and now you're riding on your stomach."

"No I'm not."

"Oh yes you are."

Ashton just stood there not moving an inch.

"You got two choices, you can lay down face first or I can put you down face first. Your choice," Symon told him.

Ashton slowly dropped to one knee, then the other before stretching out on the ground face first. Symon stepped off his horse with some rope and tied Ashton's feet together. Symon and Conaghan picked Ashton up and straddled him across the saddle of his horse. After laying him across the saddle they took a rope and tied his feet to his hands with the rope going underneath the horse to prevent him from sliding off the horse again.

"I reckon you slowed us up for the last time."

"You can't expect me to ride like this for a few hours," Ashton yelled.

"Don't bet on it."

They picked up the pace and started to ride a little harder for Kingman. Symon took the lead holding the reins of Ashton's horse behind him. After a couple hours of solid riding they could see the town a few miles out. As they continued getting closer, Symon finally started to feel at ease. They were in open spaces and he finally got the feeling that Keogh wasn't close.

Chapter 4

As the bounty hunters reached the outskirts of town, some of the residents started buzzing around the streets not believing what they were seeing. Ashton had pretty much done whatever he wanted in that town with nobody ever challenging him. Symon could see people pointing in disbelief and could hear some of the remarks, none which seemed to be pleasant.

"Why don't you get out of here," one man shouted.

"We don't like bounty hunters here," another yelled.

Symon didn't pay them any attention and focused his eyes ahead of him. After a few more moments they reached the sheriff's office. Symon stepped off his horse and looked around at the crowd that seemed to be increasing. They were keeping their distance but he noticed they were swelling in numbers. He untied Ashton from his horse and grabbed him by his belt pulling him off the animal letting him fall to the ground. He pulled Ashton back to his feet, cut the rope tying his feet together, and took him into the jail with Conaghan and Ford following. Symon saw the sheriff sitting at his desk and brought Ashton up to him.

"Brought you a prisoner, Sheriff," Symon told him.

The sheriff just sat there looking at the foursome in front of him without moving an inch. Symon seemed a little confused by his lack of action.

"Soon as you get up I'll put him in the cell there for ya," Symon said.

The sheriff stayed silent for a few more moments carefully thinking about what he wanted to say.

"Don't think I can do that, Symon," the lawman said.

A look of concern fell over Symon's face. He tilted his head a little in confusion waiting for an explanation from the sheriff.

"I don't follow," Symon confessed.

"Afraid I can't take him," the sheriff relayed.

"He's a wanted man, you're a lawman, you have to take him."

"I don't have to do anything. My only responsibility is to this town. I don't owe you a thing."

"It ain't about owing me nothing. You're wearin' a badge. You're obliged to lock a wanted man up."

"Like I said, my only obligation is to this town, and you got a few things workin' against you."

"Like what?"

"First, he's not wanted in this town. He's never done anything illegal here to not be welcomed. Second, he's been in this town quite often and there's a lot of folks on that street right now that have kinda taken a likin' to him. Now what makes you think I could hold him in here if they want him out?"

"It's your job to make sure they don't."

"Not in this town."

"What about her?" Symon asked of Ford, looking over to her.

"What about her?"

"Can you lock her up?"

"For what?"

"Attempted murder, aiding a fugitive, take your pick."

"I don't think those charges would stick in this town," the sheriff replied.

"So there's nothing you can do for us, huh?"

"Wish there was."

"Would you be able to hold them here for an hour so we could clean up a little and grab something to eat?"

"Don't think that'd be possible either."

"Had a feeling you'd say that."

Symon looked at Ashton who was smiling from ear to ear.

"I coulda told you that earlier if you decided to listen to me," Ashton smugly told him.

There was nothing Symon could do to wipe away the look of disgust he now wore on his face. He grabbed Ashton by the arm and led him back outside.

"So what're you gonna do now, Symon? You got nowhere to go," Ashton said.

Symon took his hat off and ran his hand over his head thinking about what to do next. The only option he had was to try the next town.

"What now, Brice?" Conaghan asked with concern.

"Guess we'll take 'em to Reno."

Symon put Ashton on his horse and had some words of advice for him.

"I'm gonna let you ride the rest of the way. If you start pulling the same stuff as before, you'll find yourself riding the same way as before. Understand?"

"Oh, I got ya alright, I got ya. Don't worry, I ain't gonna need to slow you up no more cause you ain't never gonna make it to Reno, I'll guarantee that," Ashton said with a smile.

The four made their way out of town with a cloud of uncertainty hanging over them. Conaghan slowed his horse up so he could ride next to Symon.

"What do you think the chances are that we'll make it to Reno?" Conaghan wondered.

"Don't rightly know."

"I have a bad feeling."

"Just stay alert. Be ready for anything."

Symon was ready for some type of conflict. He was basically just waiting for it to happen. He expected someone to jump out of a bush, or behind a tree, taking cover behind a boulder or from someplace high up. He knew they wouldn't make it to Reno without a fight. It was only a question of when it would happen. They rode for a few hours before stopping.

"Alright, we'll take a few minutes. After that, we'll walk for a spell to give the horses a breather," Symon told the group.

After walking for twenty minutes they mounted their horses again. They rode through a pass with a bunch of rocks and boulders. Suddenly a loud, booming shot rang out and Symon jumped off his horse and scurried to get next to a boulder before another shot was fired. He pulled his gun ready to return fire. He couldn't see anyone but did see some smoke rising from a nearby clump of trees. Ford wound up next to Symon, and Ashton was a few feet over. Symon then noticed that Conaghan was laying on his back with his hand over his stomach. It looked like he was bleeding pretty heavily.

"Jae, you alright?" Symon asked.

Conaghan was too weak to respond but Symon could see that he was still breathing and moving his head slightly. He was still in a vulnerable position lying out in the open. Symon holstered his weapon and darted out into the dirt where Conaghan was laying and grabbed him by the collar of his shirt and dragged him back behind the boulder for some cover. Symon quickly drew his revolver again and looked out to see if anyone was moving closer. He didn't see anything and turned his attention again to Conaghan. Symon knelt to one way and took a look at Conaghan's wound.

"It's bad isn't it?" Conaghan weakly asked.

"You'll be OK," Symon said.

Symon knew that it was bad but he wanted to try and keep the kid thinking he'd make it. He took Conaghan's gun and placed it inside his belt. He didn't want Ashton to make a play for it plus he might need the extra gun. Symon was now in a difficult position. There was no possible way he could still take in his prisoners and try to care for Conaghan at the same time. But taking them in was the least of his problems right now. He just had to figure out how to get out from being pinned down. He asked Ford to look after Conaghan while he kept an eye out for the ambusher.

"Is that your boy out there?" Symon asked Ashton.

"I would assume as much."

"How many you reckon are out there?"

"I'd say three or four. Looks like you've got yourself in a pretty tight spot."

"Looks that way."

"The only chance you have is to let me go."

"Think so?"

"You know it. That boy is dying there, and you know it. The only chance he has is if you get him to a doctor and do it right quick. Now how are you gonna do that if you're saddled with me?"

"What makes you think I care what happens to him?" Symon wondered.

"Cause he wouldn't be riding with you if you didn't. If it was me I'd leave the boy there, but you ain't me."

"Thank God for that."

A shot rang out from the trees again and Symon returned fire in that direction. He couldn't really see too much of anything other than rocks and trees. They sure picked a good spot for an ambush.

"Is that you, Keogh?" Symon yelled out.

"Sure is," Keogh shouted back.

"Looks like we got a little standoff."

"I don't quite see it like that. You got yourself a problem, but me, I got all the time in the world."

"He's got ya for sure," Ashton reminded Symon.

"Don't be so sure."

The outlaws took a few shots at Symon trying to pick him off. They didn't really have a good shot at him though. They were just trying to draw him out into a more vulnerable position.

"Symon, he needs a doctor, quickly," Ford presented.

"He's dying, Symon, you got no time to waste," Ashton convincingly said.

Symon closed his eyes and let out a big sigh knowing he had no other option but to bargain his way out of the situation.

"Do it, Symon, you know it's the only way," Ashton blurted out.

"Alright," Symon conceded.

"Now you're thinkin' smart."

Symon came up with a plan in his head that seemed pretty reasonable before presenting it to Keogh.

"Still there, Keogh?" Symon asked.

"Better believe it," he replied.

"Got a deal for ya."

"Keep talkin'."

"You can have Ashton, but I got a wounded man here, and I need time to get out of here."

"Just send Ashton over and we'll be on our way."

"You'll forgive me if I don't quite trust you."

"No hard feelings," Keogh shouted. "I wouldn't trust me either. So what do you suggest?"

"See that ridge to the east of you?"

"Yeah, I see it."

"Well when I see you and your boys on top of it, stay there for about ten minutes and I'll leave Ashton here and I'll be on my way."

"That's a long ways off. How do I know I can trust you?"

"Cause I'm not in a position to play tricks. We both know I gotta get to a doctor."

"Or I could just stay right here and wait you out."

"You could, but your friend just might wind up with a bullet in him."

"What do you say, Trist?" Keogh asked his partner.

Keogh looked to Symon to make sure he had permission to answer him, to which Symon nodded.

"Do it, Sloan. He ain't up to no tricks."

"OK. Give us a few minutes to get going."

Symon came out from behind the boulder a few minutes later and could see the outlaws leaving. He grabbed the horses which were grazing not too far away and brought them back to where everyone was and knelt beside Conaghan.

"Jae, we gotta ride, and we gotta ride hard. You're gonna be in a lot of pain, but it's the only way. Think you can make it?"

"Just get me to my horse," he whispered.

"I thought you were waiting till they got to the ridge?" Ford asked.

"Ain't got time for that."

Symon and Ford picked him up and dragged him to his horse and put him in the saddle where he barely was able to cling to it. Ashton had taken a seat and put his hands behind his head like he had no troubles in the world.

"I'm gonna need you to come with me in case I need help with him," Symon said to Ford.

Ford looked to Ashton who shrugged his shoulders like he didn't really care.

"Just help me get him there and you can be on your way after that," he told her.

"I'll do it for him, not for you."

"That suits me fine."

"I'll be seein' ya, Symon. Get ready. I'll be comin' for ya," Ashton cautioned.

"Better come shootin' cause the next time I see you I ain't asking questions or giving any warning shots. I'm just gonna blow your head off," Symon warned.

"Don't worry, I will be."

The two bounty hunters along with Ford started riding for Reno. Symon wanted to ride hard to get there quickly but he knew he couldn't push it too much cause he didn't know how much Conaghan would be able to take. He just wanted to get him to town before the outlaws caught up with them. They slowed down the pace after an hour to give the horses a little slack.

"What makes you so sure they're coming back after you?" Ford asked.

"Can't afford not to. They know they have a chance to get me before I get to town. If not, they know I'll be coming back for 'em."

"Why don't you just let them be? There's already been enough bloodshed."

"Before it was business, but it's getting personal real quick."

After slowing the pace down for an hour, Symon wanted to ride a little harder again. Only a few minutes later Conaghan slumped forward and fell off his mount. Symon turned his horse around and headed back for him.

"You alright, kid?"

"Not gonna make it," Conaghan softly conceded.

"Sure you are. You just need to rest up for a few minutes," Symon said while looking around for some shade.

Symon dragged him about twenty feet and propped him up against a tree.

"How much time will it take to get to Reno?" Ford asked while looking at Conaghan.

"Not soon enough. Probably an hour or two."

"Will he make it?"

"Not likely. Problem is he's gut-shot. Man doesn't have much of a chance when that happens."

Symon gave Conaghan a sip of water out of his canteen and took another look at his wound which was still bleeding badly. It looked like it was getting worse with each passing second.

"Brice, be honest with me. I'm not gonna make it am I?" Conaghan asked.

Symon looked to Ford like he wished she would answer the question for him.

"It's not looking too good. But just hang in there."

"I can't make it. It hurts so bad."

"You just need a few minutes to rest."

"You'll be better off without me. I'm slowing you down," he said closing his eyes.

"We either make it together or we don't make it at all, you hear me?"

Conaghan nodded his head slightly, then tilted his head back, and started breathing more heavily. He put his hand out for Symon to grab which he did.

"I just want to say thank you for letting me ride along with you," Conaghan said laboring.

"Pleasure was mine, kid."

Conaghan slowly lost grip of Symon's hand, closed his eyes, and slumped over onto his side. Symon shut his eyes and looked away momentarily, a rush of anger and sadness running through his body at the same time. He looked back at Ford whose eyes were tearing up, dabbing them for a second not wanting to cry.

"Only known him a week or so," Symon admitted. "Seemed to be as fine a young man as you could meet these days. Had a respect and decency about him…something I lost a long time ago."

Symon noticed Ford had her head down and crying into a handkerchief, which seemed odd that she'd be crying for a man who was trying to bring her and her outlaw companions in.

"You've never seen a man die before have you?" Symon wondered.

"No," she replied, shaking her head.

"Take a good look," Symon said angrily. "That's what your man has done to a dozen people."

She struggled to find any words to say and just continued looking at Conaghan.

"It's not an easy thing to get used to," Symon said sorrowfully.

Symon grabbed a small short-handle shovel and started to dig a hole for burying his partner. After the hole was big enough he placed Conaghan in it, and shoveled the dirt over top of him. He looked around and saw a few small rocks which he placed near the end of it. Hopefully somebody would be able to tell it was a grave and maybe give him a more proper wood cross or something. Symon just stood by his horse looking around.

"You don't seem to be in much of a hurry," Ford noticed.

"Can't say I am."

"Why not? You know they're coming."

"That's a fact. Only reason I was running before was cause of him. Now that he's gone, ain't got no cause for it now. I'll be ready for 'em. Besides, my horse needs a breather," he said while rubbing its nose.

"But there's five of them," Ford cautioned.

"Don't bother me none. They'll get what's coming to 'em. Shame you won't be around to see it like you wanted."

"Why won't I?"

"Cause you're free to go on your way."

"I am?"

"Yep. Ain't got no cause to keep you anymore. Much obliged to you for trying to help out with Jae."

"Thought you were taking me back to Reno for aiding a fugitive?"

"Never was my intention to do so. My only targets are Keogh and Ashton."

"So why do you do it?" Ford asked.

"Do what?"

"Bounty hunting."

"I got my reasons."

"I know, and I know it's none of my business…" she started to say before being cut off.

"You're right about that."

"Trist was right when he was talking about it, wasn't he?"

"Why don't you get going?"

"Not till I find out your reasons."

"Why does it interest you so much?"

"I'd just like to know how a man becomes as hard and ruthless as you."

"It takes years of practice," he sarcastically said.

"Afraid to answer the question?"

"You don't seem to see your boyfriend the same way as me, huh?"

"Not the side I see of him. He's always been kind and thoughtful with me."

"What about everyone else? Think he's been that way with the people he's stole from and killed?"

"Guess I never really concerned myself with how he treated others."

"Well maybe you should. It might open your eyes a little bit."

"So what happened to make you this way?" Ford asked again.

Symon looked out into the horizon wondering if he should tell her. He'd never told anyone his reasons for becoming a bounty hunter. He wasn't even sure he could explain it the way he wanted to. After a few more minutes of silence he decided to tell her. He kept looking away as he started talking.

"A few years ago I was married and had a little boy. We had a small, little spread down in Texas. Nothing big, had some horses on the outskirts of a town, but we were doing OK. Happily married, we started a nice, little family. She was pregnant with our second child. Probably a month or so away from delivering. One day they went into town to do some shopping. Just so happened that a bank robbery went down while they were there. Some shooting started and they got caught in the crossfire while in the street. Lost her and the unborn child, and my boy who was only six years old."

"I'm so sorry," Ford replied. "That's an awful thing to go through."

"It was. After that I sold the ranch and went after the men that done it. Took a few months but I got all of 'em. I swore that no other man should have to go through what I did. So I've been doing this ever since."

"I guess I can understand now. Do you ever think you could have that life again, before being a bounty hunter?"

"I reckon not. It just ain't in me anymore. I am what I've been made to be and that's just the way it is."

For some strange reason that she couldn't put her finger on Ford was actually beginning to like Symon. Maybe it was the story of him losing his family, or maybe it was that he was talking from his heart without the tough persona that he had been before. Whatever the reason was she knew that she didn't want him to wind up the same way as Conaghan.

"Well, you best get started back," Symon told her.

Ford soon after mounted her horse and started back on her way to Kingman. Symon took a seat on top of his Palomino and started riding the other direction toward Reno. Ford looked back and saw Symon riding the other way and wondered what his plan was. Symon assumed she would meet up with Ashton and Keogh on the way back. So after a half hour of riding toward Reno, Symon turned his horse around and started following Ford. He figured that if she ran into Ashton and Keogh that he could maybe pick off two or three at once if he caught them unsuspecting. He didn't think it'd take too long as they were most likely riding pretty hard after them while Symon was slowed up some by Conaghan. He just had to make sure he stayed out of sight of Ford so she didn't warn the outlaws he was on his way. Tracking her wasn't difficult at all and made up most of the ground she was leading him by. He was only a few minutes behind her. He rode through a spot that he thought would be perfect to stop and wait for them. There was some rocks that he could use for cover and a small patch of water which he figured they might stop at to let the horses drink and rest. He stepped off his horse and climbed the rocks which rose about ten feet to get a better look if someone was coming.

Ford rode for another twenty minutes before running into the Ashton and Keogh clan. The outlaw gang had been riding pretty hard to make up the ground they lost.

"Mary," Ashton shouted upon seeing her.

"Hello Trist. Hello Sloan," she offered, though she never much cared for Keogh.

She always thought Keogh was much worse than Ashton and got him riled up. Keogh seemed to have the worse temper and was more manipulative and got Ashton to do things he didn't really want to.

"How'd you escape?" Ashton wondered.

"I didn't. He let me go."

"Why'd he do that?"

"He said he didn't need me anymore," she explained.

"Which way's he headin'?" Keogh asked.

"He was heading in the direction of Reno."

"He can't be that far ahead of us with that wounded kid slowing him down," Keogh stated.

"He's not that far ahead, but he doesn't have that wounded kid slowing him down. He died," she told him with a touch of sadness.

"This shouldn't take too long then. One man against five," Keogh confidently said.

"I wouldn't underestimate him if I were you. He said he'd be ready for you."

"She's right Sloan. Symon's a tough character and no matter what the odds, he won't be easy to take down," Ashton said.

"Well he ain't gonna get the jump on me like he did with you."

"We're gonna need to water the horses soon," Ashton pointed out.

"There's a little spot up ahead where they can rest for a few minutes," Ford told them.

"Good. Let's ride," Keogh told the group.

They rode for the spot that Ford had told them about to freshen up the horses. Symon saw the group coming and got down from the rocks. They were only a few minutes away from him so he grabbed his Remington rifle from his horse and waited for his opponents to appear.

He heard the group's horses as they came closer and then stopped as they drank the water. Symon peered out from behind a rock brought his rifle up to eye level ready to explode. He wanted to try and hit Ashton or Keogh first but they were blocked by the other members of the gang. He opened fire hitting one member in the chest knocking him off his horse then fired another round hitting a man in the back of his shoulder. He took aim at the man again but his next shot missed. All the members of the group started scattering. Ashton, Keogh, and Ford took off hard while the other two took cover for themselves.

"I'm not really interested in you boys," Symon yelled. "If you don't want to meet your end, I suggest you grab your horses and take off. You'll get no resistance from me."

They chose to reply by the firing of their guns. They were the kind who would rather die than run away from a fight.

"Alright you sons of bitches, prepare to meet your maker," Symon shouted.

He fired a few more rounds at the men without doing any damage. He reloaded just in time to see the one trying to move into a better position. He fired a couple shots as the man was running hitting him in both of his kneecaps which shattered upon impact. He was lying on the ground moaning in excruciating pain. The man that was wounded in his shoulder took off running to get a spot closer to Symon. Symon saw him out of the corner of his eye but couldn't really get a clear shot at him. He decided to move around the other side of the rocks and come up behind the man. The outlaw started firing at where he thought Symon was without any return fire. He thought maybe he hit Symon since he wasn't firing any return rounds. He came out behind his cover and started walking closer to where he believed Symon to be. Symon had come full circle around him and was approaching him from behind.

"Looks like you made the wrong choice, friend," Symon simply stated.

The man instantly stopped upon hearing Symon's voice knowing he had the upper hand. He tried the only chance he had. He swung around quickly with his Colt revolver ready to fire but Symon blew a hole in his chest instantly knocking him backwards before he could get his shot off. Symon approached him to make sure he was dead but nobody could survive a bullet from that close range. He once again heard the other man moaning and went up to him.

"Just put me out of my misery," the man painfully said, looking up at him.

Symon brought his rifle up to finish the man off then a second later brought it back down to his side.

"Nope, don't believe I will," he said to himself.

"You're not gonna leave me out here like this for the buzzards are you?"

"The thought occurred to me."

Symon noticed his handgun laying a few feet away and walked over to pick it up. He unloaded all the bullets except for one. He spun the chamber and handed it to the fellow.

"Got one bullet," Symon said tossing on the ground next to him.

"Much obliged."

Symon grabbed the reins of his horse and mounted to go after the rest of the group. A minute later he heard a shot ring out from where he had just left ending that outlaw's life. He stopped for a second when hearing the shot and looked to the ground beside him almost as if he wanted to look back. He shrugged it off though and picked up the tracks of the outlaws quickly and followed them for a few minutes before realizing they were heading back to Kingman. The town would hide them if that's what they wanted, but he didn't much care. He would find them no matter what it took. He didn't even care about the reward money anymore. He was doing it to avenge Conaghan's death. Ashton, Keogh, and Ford arrived at Kingman a short time later and went to the sheriff's office. When seeing him, they let him know that Symon was coming and to do something about him.

"Symon's on his way here, you gotta do something about him," Keogh told him.

"Like what?" the sheriff asked.

"Why don't you arrest him?" Ashton asked.

"For what?"

"Murder," Ashton said.

"Yeah, he murdered a couple of our friends back there," Ashton chimed in. "You gotta lock him up and put him behind bars where he belongs."

"Alright, I'll see what I can do."

The outlaws then went over to the saloon and had a drink while waiting for Symon to come in. Now they were in their town and they felt comfortable even if Symon showed up for them. They had a dozen friends who would back them up in a second if some gunplay started or some trouble started. Symon knew it too. As he approached the edge of the town he had his head on a swivel looking in every direction almost waiting for some trouble to find him. He trotted towards the center of town when he saw the sheriff come out of his office and waved at him to come closer.

"Symon," he yelled.

Symon wasn't sure if he wanted to talk to the lawman but decided to go over to hear what he had to say. He dismounted his horse and led it over to where the sheriff was standing. He didn't want to stay sitting on his horse and be a target for someone who might decide to shoot him in the back. The horse gave him a little bit of cover.

"Something you want to tell me?" Symon asked.

"Looks like I'm gonna have to arrest you."

"For what?" Symon asked, looking him up and down.

"The murder of a couple men just outside of town," the sheriff replied.

"That's not your jurisdiction. You couldn't make it stick if you tried."

"Nevertheless, I'm gonna have to lock you up and wire for the U.S. Marshall."

Symon simply shook his head in disagreement.

"I don't want any trouble from you, Symon."

"I wouldn't start something I wasn't prepared to finish if I was you," Symon warned him.

"Are you gonna come easy?"

"Ain't comin' at all."

Symon moved his right hand to the handle of his Colt revolver that was strapped to his leg. The sheriff noticed and gulped not really wanting to get into a gunfight with him. He let his hand down slowly, waiting for Symon to make his play. Symon menacingly stared at him figuring the sheriff would either back down or be killed.

"Just tell me where they are," Symon asked him.

The sheriff was starting to lose his nerve. The main reason he was the sheriff there was because the town never really needed him. Most things were taken care of on their own and he never really had to do much. And that's the way he liked it. Gunplay and showdowns weren't really something that appealed to him.

"Over in the saloon," he said, nodding his head in that direction.

Then the sheriff backed away and went inside his office. Symon walked over to the saloon and looked inside before going in. He scanned the room and noticed Ford sitting at a table by herself in the corner. He walked in and noticed that not a single head turned towards him. They all knew he was there though, they were expecting him. Ford saw him walking up to her table and pushed out a seat for him. He sat down and poured himself a drink with the bottle of whiskey that was sitting on the table.

"Didn't expect to see you so soon," she told him.

"How so?"

"Looked like you were on your way to Reno."

"That was my intention. I knew you'd tell them I was heading there so I doubled back and trailed you, and just waited for them to show up."

Ford continued staring straight ahead.

"Where are they?" Symon asked.

"Upstairs."

Symon was about to push his chair out to stand up when Ford grabbed his hand.

"I wouldn't go up there if I were you," Ford informed him.

"Why?"

"They're waiting for you. As soon as you go up there they'll gun you down. You won't have a chance. Plus all these fools in here would never let you get out even if you did somehow manage to kill them."

"Appreciate the advice, but why are you warning me? Seems somewhat strange."

"You deserve a chance."

"Seems like a departure from your previous views of me," he noted.

"Yeah, well, maybe my views are starting to change."

Symon had another drink trying to figure out his next move. It looked like he'd have to wait a little bit to extract his revenge on them.

"I have to warn you about the sheriff," Ford blurted out. "They cooked up a plan where they'd arrest you for murdering the rest of the group and lock you up. They'd most likely end up hanging you or shooting you in the process."

"I know. I've already had a little chat with the sheriff. We're on friendly terms now."

"I guess that was one of the reasons I'm warning you. I didn't much care for what they were planning," she confessed.

"Well, I'm obliged to you."

"So what are you gonna do?" she asked.

"No idea."

Symon knew what he had to do but he was trying to think of some other way. The only option he had now was to leave town and wait. It wouldn't have been the first time he waited an outlaw out until the time was right, but in this case, he didn't want to do it. He wanted them now. But in cases where his head and heart were telling him two different things he usually listened to his head. This time would be no different. He'd have to leave town and pick up their trail another time. He told Ford to deliver a message for him.

"Tell them that I won't forget 'em. It might be a year from now, but I'll be back."

"I'll tell them."

"Well, good luck to ya," Symon wished her.

"Same to you. Stay healthy."

Symon left the saloon, mounted his horse, and rode out of town without much fanfare. Contrary to what he told Ford, he had no intention of waiting a year to get Ashton and Keogh. He didn't even plan on waiting a week.

Ford had gone upstairs where they had a few rooms and met with Ashton and Keogh to let them know that Symon had gone.

"What'd he have to say?" Keogh wondered.

"Just said it might be a year from now but he'll be back," Ford responded.

"It won't take him no year, I guarantee that," Ashton chimed in. "He's probably waiting for us outside of town right now."

Keogh ran his hand over his face, stroking his beard trying to figure out Symon's next move.

"He don't strike me as the type who'd just give up like that," Keogh said.

"He's a stubborn one. He's out there. He's out there," Ashton stated.

"So what do you plan to do?" Ford asked.

"Which way out of town was he heading?" Keogh asked.

"I didn't notice," Ford replied.

Keogh gave her a violent backhand slap that sent her to the floor.

"You only had one job out there and that was to make sure he came up to find us so we could ambush him or find out where he was heading and you didn't do either one," Keogh shouted at her.

Ford didn't respond to him and looked up to Ashton expecting him to help her in some way. He just stood there not seemingly bothered by what Keogh did to her.

"We could just stay here for a while," Ashton offered.

"I ain't bottling myself up in some room for weeks or months just cause some bounty hunter's out there lookin' for me," Keogh told him. "I ain't afraid of a fight with him. I'll bury the son of a bitch."

"We could split up and take our chances. He could only follow one of us," Ashton countered.

They decided to go their separate ways for a little while and meet back at their cabin in three months. If one of them didn't show up then the other would know what happened. Symon took up camp a little north of town hoping they'd go in that direction. He didn't figure they'd go back to their cabin since he knew where it was, and going in Reno's direction seemed like a bad choice since they already tried that. So he figured they'd either go north or south.

Chapter 5

Symon kept a lookout for a few days waiting for a sign that one of them was heading in his direction. The thought occurred to him that maybe they were staying in town for a while. Maybe he had spooked them to the point where they didn't feel comfortable going anywhere and would stay where they felt relatively safe. He was not someone who liked to react to what others did and was tired of waiting.

Symon decided to head back towards Kingman to either pick up their trail if they were on the move or catch them in surprise. He kept an eye out for any tracks on the way to town but he didn't see any signs that they went in that direction. As he rode into town he felt a few fingers being pointed at him. He stayed alert in case any wandering guns started firing. Symon noticed the sheriff sitting in front of his office just watching him ride by.

He stopped his horse in front of the saloon and walked in expecting anything. Unlike his last time in there, everybody turned their head and watched his movements, surprised that he was there again. Symon walked up to the bar and summoned the bartender to his location.

"So where are they?" Symon asked.

"Who?" the bartender replied.

Symon took his arm and cleared the bar of the glasses in front of him letting them violently shatter on the floor. He then reached across the bar and grabbed the bartender by the collar pulling him over the bar.

"I'm tired of playing games with people in this town. You better start talking and telling me what I want to hear," Symon angrily said.

Just as the bartender was about to say something, Ford entered the bar through a side door.

"Let him go, Brice," she told him as she walked up to him.

Symon let the man go at her request. Ford led him to a table where they sat down.

"Why did you come back here?" Ford asked.

"Same reasons as before."

"I thought you said it might take a year."

"Changed my mind."

"Well they didn't believe it either."

"So where are they?"

"They left town."

"Where'd they go?"

"I don't know."

Symon simply gave her a look of disbelief. She always knew their whereabouts. Ford knew that he didn't believe that answer but she swore it was the truth.

"They didn't tell me where they were going, I swear they didn't," she confessed.

"What do you know?"

"They split up."

"Why?"

"They figured you couldn't follow both of them. It didn't really make much sense to me. I would think they'd rather have strength in numbers but they didn't seem to be thinking very clearly."

"Good. That puts it in my favor."

"Anybody traveling with them?" Symon wanted to know.

"Nope. All by themselves."

"It does seem a bit strange but I guess nobody ever said they were scholars."

"You could just wait here for them if you really wanted to."

"Why's that?"

"They said they'd meet back at the cabin in three months," she told.

"I'm not much good at waiting."

"It'd be a lot easier than going after them wouldn't it?"

"I'm impatient."

"I've noticed."

"I'm obliged to you for the information but why are you telling me all this?" Symon wondered. "Seems to me that you're setting your boyfriend up for a fall."

"I'm through with him. I hope he gets what's coming to him."

"What happened?" Symon curiously asked.

"After you left the last time they were unhappy that I didn't get you upstairs or find out where you were heading. And they let me know it."

"That where you got that bruise on your cheek from?" Symon noticed.

Ford put her hand up to her cheek. She had tried to cover it up with makeup and did a pretty good job. Most didn't look closely enough to notice the mark but Symon was pretty good at noticing things others missed. Ford nodded at his assertion.

"Why else are you helping me? Even before that, you could have sent me up there knowing what would've happened?" Symon questioned.

"I don't know. Maybe what you said about your family had an effect on me."

Symon said goodbye to Ford again and went on his way after his targets. He went south and within a few hours had picked up the tracks of a single horse. It must've been about a day old. It had to be either Ashton or Keogh. He followed them until he came to a stream when they suddenly stopped. He led his horse downstream splashing through the water figuring that they were trying to hide their tracks. Symon went about thirty yards before noticing horse prints in the dirt coming out of the stream. He rode at a pretty good pace for the rest of the day trying to catch up to the man in front of him.

Once nightfall hit he made camp. He made a small fire, ate, drank coffee and stared into the crackling flames. His mind raced back to when he owned a ranch working with his horses and seeing his son watch him from behind the fences. He remembered how great his wife's cooking smelled. Then his thoughts turned to him standing over the graves where they were buried. He wasn't sure if he should try forgetting the images that seemed to be burned in his mind permanently or if he should try to put them behind him and move on. Then Conaghan's last moments began creeping their way into his head. He felt that if he told him no when he asked to tag along then he'd still be alive today. A sense of guilt and responsibility came over him.

Symon finally was able to shake loose the images that haunted him and bed down for the night. He kept his firearms close to him in case he had any late night intruders, whether it be two or four legged. Luckily the night came and went without any problems interrupting it. Symon just had a cup of coffee in the morning as he wanted to get a quick start on the day. He picked up the tracks again and they seemed to be getting fresher as the day went on. He was definitely gaining ground on whoever he was following. The tracks were leading into the hills where some outlaws had a tendency to try and disappear. He kicked his horse to ride harder to get even closer and he soon figured that he was only about an hour behind judging from the horse prints.

As Symon rode through the hills he kept a sharp eye out as he knew that an ambush could happen at any time. He couldn't be sure if he was actually gaining ground or if the person ahead of him was slowing down and letting him catch up. Symon reached the top of one of the hills and looked towards the bottom and saw a rider on a Paint horse. He squinted to see if he could make out who it was but he was still too far away, so he sprinted down to the bottom of the hill to catch up to him. The man Symon was chasing heard something behind him and turned around to see Symon come charging down. The man spurred his horse on to avoid what was coming after him. He tried to outrun Symon but his horse lost its balance and dumped the rider on top of him. Symon came flying in and stopped just in front of the man with his rifle drawn. He left his finger on the trigger as he waited for the man to get to his feet. As soon as the man rose to his feet his eyes bulged out seeing that he was about to get shot. But once Symon saw his face he took his finger off the trigger and put the rifle away. It wasn't Ashton or Keogh. He'd been following the wrong trail.

"I do somethin' to you, mister?" the man asked him with a puzzled look on his face.

"Thought you were someone else," Symon replied. "My apologies."

Symon turned his horse around and rode away frustrated that he had the wrong man. He rode back towards Kingman to try and pick up another set of tracks. Even though he was not happy following the wrong man he still knew he had the advantage. He could afford to make a mistake like that cause he knew even if he didn't find them, he knew where they'd be in three months. They couldn't afford to make any mistakes as it could cost them their life.

When Symon reached the outskirts of Kingman he found another set of tracks leading west to Reno. He couldn't be sure if it was one of the men he was looking for, especially after going after the wrong man before, but he didn't have any other options. He was at least a few days behind Ashton and Keogh wherever they went. This time he decided that he wasn't going to rush into anything. He'd stay on their trail good enough but if it took a week or two weeks to catch up to them he was OK with that. The longer it took him to find them than they might start getting nervous wondering where he was and make a crucial mistake.

He rode for a few days still picking up the trail of a lone rider. He was keeping his eyes focused on the ground when he looked up and noticed a couple men riding towards him. They didn't seem to be in any kind of hurry so he didn't think they were who he was after or any kind of threat, just the same he pulled his Colt in and out of the holster just to make sure it didn't stick in case he needed it in a hurry. As the strangers approached, Symon noticed one of them was wearing a lawman's badge. Symon stopped his horse as the two men came closer.

"Howdy," the lawman greeted him.

"Howdy Sheriff," Symon replied.

"Actually I'm a U.S. Deputy Marshal," he informed.

"What can I do for ya?"

"Looking for a man. Wondering if maybe you seen him?"

"What's he look like?"

"Can't say there's anything special about him. In his 30's I'd say, bout 5'8, slender, black hair, riding a Paint horse," the lawman explained.

"A paint horse?"

"Yeah. Sound familiar?"

"It might. Ran into a fella a few days ago who matched that description."

"Where was he?"

"Up in the hills."

"Was he camped up there?"

"Just riding."

"How 'bout you? Where you heading?" the lawman wondered.

"Not heading anyplace. Looking for some fellas. Come across anybody on your way here?"

"Can't say that we have. Saw a man in the distance a day or so back but didn't get close enough to see his face. Who is it that you're after?"

"Trist Ashton and Sloan Keogh."

"You set your sights pretty big don't ya?"

"I reckon so. So this rider you saw, how do you know it wasn't the man you were looking for if you didn't see his face?"

"Cause I could see his horse. And it wasn't a Paint."

"Maybe he changed horses."

"Nah, not him. He loves that horse more than anything. The only way he'd ride a different horse is if that one died."

"Oh."

"Why you after Sloan and Keogh? You a bounty hunter?"

"That I am."

"I thought so. What's your name?"

"Brice Symon."

"I've heard of you. Your reputation precedes you. I have to say that I pictured you as a much bigger man from your reputation."

"Reality usually isn't how people say it is."

"Really think you can handle Ashton and Keogh by yourself?" he asked.

"No question about it. Right now they've split up though," Symon confided. "They went in two different directions."

"Well I wish you luck. Be careful they're not setting you up," the lawman cautioned.

"How you figure?"

"Maybe one is leading you out so the other one can come in from behind and box you in."

"Can't say it crossed my mind. Although I guess that would be one explanation as to why they split up instead of staying together."

"You never know. Just be aware."

"Appreciate the advice."

"You bet. Well, good luck to ya."

"Much obliged."

Symon picked up the trail of the rider the Deputy Marshal was telling him about. He followed it for a couple days till he was almost on top of him. As far as Symon could tell he was only maybe an hour or so behind him. He knew it was one of the men he was after. The feeling in his gut told him that there'd be no mistake this time around. As he moved closer to coming in contact with him, Symon wondered if maybe it was too easy. Maybe the man was slowing up waiting for Symon to come along and ambush him. As he rode along, Symon made sure to keep an eye out for any spots that'd be good for bushwhacking. Symon pulled out his rifle as he rode along, holding it loosely in his right hand as he held the reins of his horse in the other. He was increasingly getting an uneasy feeling with each passing second.

As nightfall came upon him, Symon decided to make camp for the night. He figured he could catch up to whomever he was trailing in the morning. Although he was so close and anxious to find out the man he was near, he wanted to make sure he had a clear view of everything. Darkness could conceal too many hiding places. He wouldn't let his anticipation override his experience no matter how tempting it might be. He slept with his rifle by his side, like he usually did, just in case anyone decided to surprise him in the middle of the night. It turned out to be an uneventful evening however.

Symon woke up at daybreak and had a cup of coffee. He was feeling too anxious to really eat anything though. As he was breaking camp and getting his horse saddled he heard a couple shots ring out. They were close but far enough away to know that they weren't coming in his direction. No, someone out there had a fight on their hands. He quickly saddled his horse and went in the direction the gunfire was coming from. He rode quickly and with rifle in hand expecting to see some type of action.

Symon saw smoke rising in the air only a few minutes from where he was riding. He cautiously moved forward ready for whatever was about to happen. Probably for anything other than what he was about to see. He couldn't believe what he saw.

"I'll be damned," he said to himself.

He was disappointed in what he was witnessing. He saw Trist Ashton laying face first on the ground with three men standing over top of him. As he approached the men they turned around ready for some more action. Symon put his hands up to signal he wasn't there for trouble. Symon sized up the three men before him and didn't figure they were of much threat to him. They didn't look like gunfighters. One of the men was short, one had a full black beard, and the other was a rather large, heavyset man.

"Just hold on fellas, I'm not here to help him," he told the group.

Upon hearing Symon's voice, Ashton turned his head in Symon's direction and smiled. His smile soon turned to laughter.

"What the hell you laughin' at?" the short man asked him, giving Ashton a little kick to the shoulder.

"Looks like they beat you to it, Symon," Ashton yelled out.

"Symon? You Brice Symon?" the bearded cowboy asked.

"Yep."

"He's ours, Symon. We found him and you ain't gonna take him from us."

"I've been tracking him for some time now," Symon pointed out, hoping he could pry the prisoner away from them.

"We don't care if you've been tracking him for years. We found him so we're taking him in. You would do the same thing if you was us."

"I guess I would at that."

"We don't want no trouble from you. We know your reputation but we ain't feared of ya."

"You boys bounty hunters, or you just happened along this little treasure here?"

"We just been drifting. I remembered seeing his face on a wanted poster few weeks back," the bearded cowboy explained.

"Don't let 'em take me, Symon. You been tracking me for a while, you deserve to take me in," Ashton shouted.

"I can see you still got that mouth on you."

"Why would he want you to take him in?" one of the drifters asked Symon.

"No reason. He just likes to talk a lot. Tries to get inside your head."

The three men pulled Ashton up and tied his hands together.

"Bringing back memories for you?" Symon asked the outlaw.

"Yeah, kinda missed it," Ashton said jokingly.

"Where you figure on takin' him?" Symon asked the newfound bounty hunters.

"Why, figurin' on tailin' us?" the heavyset cowboy wondered.

"Nope. Just curious."

"You ain't figurin' on tryin' come at us from behind and take him away from us are ya?"

"Wouldn't dream of it. After all, there's three of ya," he said sarcastically.

"I reckon we'll be takin' him to Kingman. That's the closest town from here," the one cowboy stated.

"Wouldn't recommend it," Symon told him.

"Why's that?"

"First off, he's got a lot of friends there. Second, the sheriff won't take him."

"How can he not take him? He's a lawman, he's gotta take him."

"I hear he's a pretty stubborn man. Don't think you'll get paid taking him there."

"Maybe he'll just need a little persuadin' if you know what I mean. We can be pretty convincin' when we're a mind to it," the bearded one said.

"I can see that. Well if you're mind's made up…"Symon said, before being interrupted.

"You ain't seriously gonna leave me with these deadbeats, are ya?" Ashton asked him.

"Well they did get to you first."

"These shave tails couldn't lead me to my horse without needin' directions."

"They seem like nice, upright citizens to me. You boys gonna let him talk to you that way?" Symon told the men, trying to provoke them.

One of the cowboys gave Ashton a punch across his face staggering him to his knees. Symon had a little chuckle at Ashton's misfortune. The initial disappointment he felt at not getting to Ashton first had disappeared now. He knew he would wind up with another chance at it. He knew there was no way they'd be dropping him off at Kingman. He wasn't sure if they'd make it that far or if something would happen once they got to town, but one way or another, he knew these tinhorns would never collect that bounty.

"Well, I wish you boys luck," Symon told the group. "You boys need me to tag along?"

"I think we're man enough to handle one man," the heavyset one said.

"Suit yourself," Symon said, bidding the men goodbye with a tip to his hat.

"Don't you wanna know what our names are?" the short cowboy asked.

"Nope. Doesn't interest me," Symon replied, kicking his horse into a gallop.

Symon rode away from the men for about ten minutes before reaching higher ground and stopping. He looked back and could see the group starting on their journey to town. He waited there for a few more minutes before following them. He was planning on staying just far enough behind them to where he wouldn't be seen, but close enough to where he could get a piece of Ashton or Keogh if he were to show up. Or if they actually made it to town he could see what would transpire. After riding for a few hours Ashton couldn't keep his tongue in any longer.

"You boys realize you're being followed don't ya?"

The three cowboys pulled up on their horses and turned around to see if Ashton was right.

"I don't see nothin'," one stated.

"Course you don't," Ashton replied. "And you ain't goin' to either till it's too late."

"How do you know?" another one asked.

"I just know. It's either my partner or it's Symon but you can bet it's one of them."

"How far back you figure?"

"Not too far. I'd guess less than an hour or so."

That was all the cowboys needed to hear before coming to the conclusion they needed to make a hard ride to town. They spurred their horses on realizing they had to make Kingman quickly before whoever was behind them caught up to them. Ashton didn't say anything else but was somewhat amused by his captors. He knew it was Symon behind them but he wasn't sure what he was planning. All he knew was that Symon was planning something. He sure wasn't gonna let some greenhorns take someone he had been after. So Ashton wanted to get these fellas riled up to get to Kingman quickly. He didn't know what Symon was up to but he knew that if he got to town first he'd be safe there.

As Symon followed he could tell the men he was pursuing started to ride a little harder. He wasn't sure if they figured out he was following or if they just wanted to get to town faster but he kept up the pace with them. Ashton and the three cowboys arrived at Kingman after dark. The streets were empty until they got to the middle of town. Then people started to realize what was happening and started to file out into the street. The sheriff came out of his office and stood in front of it waiting for the group to come to him. He knew trouble was coming.

Chapter 6

The sheriff spoke up as the group of men came closer to him.

"Can I help you boys?" the sheriff asked.

"Got a wanted man here for you, Sheriff," one cowboy stated.

The group started to dismount their horses but the sheriff interrupted them before they swung their legs over their saddles.

"I wouldn't bother if I was you," the sheriff told the men.

The cowboys stopped the motion of getting off their horses, their legs sticking up in the air over their saddles in unison, surprised that the lawman wasn't more welcoming. They sat back in their saddles and looked at each other unsure of what to do next.

"How do we go about getting the reward for this man?" the big man asked.

"You don't. Least not here anyways."

"How's that so, sheriff? You're a lawman. You're obliged to take him."

"I ain't obliged to do nothin'. I said you ain't leavin' him here," the lawman sternly told them.

"So what would you suggest we do?" the short bounty hunter asked.

"Well if you boys look to your left you'll see the edge of town. Once you see that last building...just keep riding. Don't much care where you go after that."

Upon hearing the sheriff's words Ashton just started quietly laughing. His laughter quickly subsided however once he looked to his right and saw a single rider approaching. He knew it was Symon. It became clearer as the rider calmly approached. The man wasn't in any hurry. Everyone turned in the rider's direction once they all realized that it was Symon.

"Well this'll be interestin'," Ashton whispered to no one in particular.

Symon stopped once he got to the cluster of men around the sheriff's office. He stayed on his horse surveying the situation.

"Something I can do for you, Symon?" the sheriff offered, not expecting to see him again.

"Nope."

"Why are you here?"

"Just visiting."

"You have an interest in what's going on here?" the sheriff questioned.

"No more than anybody else that's here. Just curious as to what's gonna happen."

"Well it looks like you're wasting your time cause nothin's gonna happen."

"Told you boys you'd have a hard time if you came this way," Symon told the three cowboys.

Ashton was amused by all the fuss they were making over him. But he was a little worried about Symon. He wasn't too much concerned over the cowboys as they weren't too experienced and he figured he could either kill them or escape from them at some point. But he'd have a hard time doing that if Symon kept following which he figured he probably would. Ashton figured his best chance was if he somehow stayed right there in town.

"I have an idea, Sheriff," Ashton stated.

"What's that?"

"Since there's all this commotion over me, why don't you hold me in your jail and hand over the reward money to these here fellas?"

Both Symon and the Sheriff looked curiously at Ashton not quite believing what they heard come out of his mouth. He was actually asking to be put in jail. Symon knew he was up to some trick.

"You're offering to go to jail?" Symon asked.

"Why not? Maybe I've had my fill of runnin' around. Maybe I'm tired of people like you chasin' after me."

"I find that hard to believe."

"That doesn't surprise me a bit, Symon. You're a man who don't believe in much of nothin' as far as I can tell," Ashton replied.

"I believe in what I know. And I know that you're a man who would do or say anything to save his own hide."

Ashton turned his attention back to the sheriff.

"Ready to take me in?"

"Get off your horse," the lawman regretfully told him, not sure of what he was planning but knowing he probably wouldn't like it.

The three cowboys started to dismount their horses again, before they were once again interrupted by the sheriff.

"No need for you boys to get down. You ain't getting' no reward money tonight. Only thing open now is the saloon and hotel. You'll get your money in the morning."

Symon took his right foot out of his stirrup to get off his horse, almost waiting to see if the sheriff would have the guts to tell him not to get off. He looked at the lawman the entire time till both of his feet were planted firmly on the dirt street. The sheriff already knew that Symon meant business and had no desire to get into any type of conflict with him. He would deal with him if he had to but preferred to just avoid him if at all possible. Symon walked up to the lawman, who had grabbed Ashton by the arm, ready to lead him into the jail.

"What are you doing?" the sheriff asked.

"Just for peace of mind, you don't mind if I watch you put him into a cell, do you?" Symon countered.

"I suppose not."

The sheriff took Ashton inside and grabbed the keys to the cells with Symon walking behind them. The sheriff unlocked one of the cells, untied Ashton's hands and placed him in the cell, locking the door behind him.

"Satisfied?" the sheriff asked, turning to Symon.

"For the moment."

"Leaving town now?" the sheriff asked eagerly, hoping he'd say yes.

"I'll stick around a day or so."

"Why? Now that Ashton's locked up you got no reason to stay here."

"If you think for one second that I believe that he's gonna stay in that jail you got another thing coming to you."

"Well what do you think is gonna happen?" the lawman wondered.

"I'm not quite sure yet. At the moment I'm figurin' that someone will break him out, or you'll let him out. That sound about right?"

"Well if a bunch of men come bustin' through this jail wanting to let him go, I sure ain't gonna take a bullet for him."

Symon simply looked at him wondering how a lawman had degenerated to the point where he didn't care about the duties he swore to uphold.

"Don't look at me with so much contempt. I do what this town wants me to do. I protect those that live here. Those are my only interests. Whether they're law-abiding, outlaws, or whatever, as long as the town wants them to stay...they'll stay. And no outsider will change that."

"I can see that."

"I guess you're figurin' on staying for the night?" the sheriff asked.

"I believe I will. Just so you're of understandin', I'm a light sleeper, and anybody who comes messing around my door will likely find a bullet coming through it," Symon warned.

"I don't suspect you'll find anyone snooping around your door."

Symon went over to the saloon to get a few drinks before heading to the hotel. He noticed the three cowboys sitting at a table playing cards with each other and having drinks. He gave a nod to them as he passed them on the way to the bar. As soon as he ordered a drink he saw Mary Ford come into the saloon. She noticed him right away and walked up to him.

"I'm surprised to see you again so soon," Ford told him.

"Not as surprised as I am."

"Well what are you doing here?"

"Ashton's in jail."

"I know. So why are you still here though? Shouldn't you be out after Keogh now?"

"Not till something happens with Ashton."

"What do you mean?"

"You know as well as I do that he ain't staying in that jail."

She knew he was right. She knew the town well enough and knew the men well enough to know that Ashton would not still be sitting in jail come morning.

"So what are you gonna do, just wait till something happens?" Ford asked.

"The thought occurred to me."

"But that could take a while."

"I don't think it'll take quite that long. Most likely a day or two at the most."

"Well if you're planning on staying here you better be careful and watch yourself. Trist still has a lot of friends here."

"I know. But right now I don't think I'm what they're worried about."

"Why not?"

"Cause I didn't bring him in. They did," Symon said, nodding over to the cowboys at the table.

"What do you think will happen, Brice?"

"I'm thinkin' that somebody's gonna go release Ashton from jail before morning hits."

They continued talking for an hour or so before the cowboys started getting a little loud from drinking so much. They were really taking to the bottle. Some of the other patrons in the saloon were starting to get a little annoyed with their behavior. They started singing loudly while they were drinking and playing cards.

"Why don't you guys shut your hole?" one cowboy asked a few tables away.

"Why don't you go crawl under your rock?" the short bounty hunter replied with a slight slur in his speech.

"What'd you say?" the cowboy asked again angrily, this time standing up, knocking his chair over behind him.

"I said you're an ugly lookin' jackass," he replied again, the whiskey making him talk without fear.

The insulted cowboy slowly walked closer to the table ready for some gunplay.

"When you go insultin' a man like that you ought to be ready to back it up," he told the bounty hunter, his hand on the grip of his revolver.

The short cowboy realized that the man he was insulting was ready for a gunfight. He wasn't intending for his words to lead up to that though. He started trying to talk his way out of it once he saw the man in front of him meant business.

"Listen friend, why don't I buy you a drink and we'll forget all about it?"

"I don't drink with the likes of bounty hunters."

"We're not bounty hunters."

"You just brought Ashton in, didn't ya?"

"Yeah, but we weren't intending to. We just happened across him."

"You brought him in for money. That makes you bounty hunters. And that makes you scum. Now you best be standin' up or I'll plug you where you're sittin'."

Symon and Ford looked on anxiously to see the result.

"I know him, Brice, he's not too bad with a gun. You should do something. He'll probably kill that cowboy. He won't stand a chance."

"Ain't my fight," Symon told her. "Besides, it's of his own doing. When a man's in an unwelcoming environment he's got to know there's a time when you ought to sit nice and tight, real quiet like. Right now nobody really cares about me being here and I intend to keep it that way. And besides that, he's got two friends sitting right next to him. If they're of mind, they'll stop it."

"This isn't going to turn out good."

"Not likely."

"So what's it gonna be bounty boy?" the gunman asked, ready for his opponent to throw down.

The room fell silent for a minute while everyone watched expecting some gunplay. The newly appointed bounty hunter nervously debated in his mind whether he should draw on the gunslinger in front of him. He finally decided that he would take on the belligerent cowboy. He jumped up while simultaneously grabbing his gun pulling it from his holster but barely had it cleared before he was knocked backwards from a bullet to the chest, his leg still hanging over a portion of the chair. The town gunman easily outdrew the slightly drunk man. The other bounty hunters checked on their friend who didn't have a breath left in him.

"Now let that be a lesson to ya," the town gunslinger told the remaining members of the group as he holstered his pistol.

Symon still kept a close eye on the situation as he wasn't sure it was over with. Something was telling him there was more action to come. He noticed the bearded cowboy grab the arm of the heavyset one who shrugged him off. As the town gunman reached his table he heard a voice call out to him.

"Think you can do that again?" the heavyset cowboy yelled out.

The gunman turned around to look at his foe.

"I'm sure of it," he stated.

Everyone in the saloon cleared out of their paths and clung to the walls to the side of them.

"Brice," Ford started to say before he grabbed her and led her to the wall.

The two men locked in the showdown stared at each other, each waiting for the other to make a move. Finally the heavyset cowboy reached for his gun which stuck inside the holster. He looked down and reached his other hand down to remove his pistol and just as he looked back up a bullet lodged into his stomach causing him to drop to both knees. Holding his heavily bleeding stomach with his left hand he finally was able to remove his gun with his right hand but was unable to use it. Just as he raised the pistol up he was knocked over with another fatal shot in his chest.

"I told you he was pretty good," Ford said to Symon.

"Not too bad. He's a might handy with that thing."

"Be watchful of him."

"I intend to."

"You want your shot," the gunslinger asked the remaining cowboy.

The man simply shook his head no. He knew he was no match for the man after seeing his two comrades go down rather easily. A few minutes later the sheriff walked in and saw the two dead bodies lying on the floor.

"What happened here?" the sheriff asked the room.

"Self defense," the gunslinger stood up and told him.

"You do these?" the sheriff asked, pointing to one of the bodies.

"Sure did. Like I said, it was a fair fight."

The sheriff looked to the bearded cowboy to get his take on what went down.

"What do you say?"

"It was fair," the cowboy answered solemnly.

The sheriff glanced around the room again to check for somebody else's view.

"Symon?"

"Like they both said, it was a fair fight."

"Alright then. I'll fetch the undertaker."

The crowd settled down and everything began to get back to normal. Symon and Ford sat back down at a table. The bearded cowboy came over and sat down as well.

"Something I can do for you?" Symon asked wondering what he wanted.

"You saw what happened."

"What's your point?"

"They're gonna do whatever it takes so they don't have to pay a bounty. They'll kill the both of us."

"You maybe. Not me. Besides, I didn't bring him in, you did."

"I'll split the money with you."

"Not interested."

"Why not?"

"I have my own selfish reasons."

"They're gonna try and kill me."

"I doubt it."

"You saw what they just did."

"Your friends got in over their head. The short one shot his mouth off and the fat one thought he was something more than he was. I wouldn't recommend you making the same mistake. You just go about your business and you'll live to see another town after this one."

"You think so?"

"Yeah. But I wouldn't count on seeing any of that reward money. He won't be in that jail by the time you go to collect," Symon warned.

"You don't seem too concerned about it."

"Can't say that I am."

"Why not?"

"Like I said, I have my own reasons."

The cowboy left and went to the hotel to retire for the night. He figured the best chance he had of staying out of trouble in the unwelcoming town was to just stay out of sight.

"You hear anything about Keogh?" Symon asked Ford.

Ford looked around to see if there were any wandering ears listening in, which there were none.

"From what I hear he's hiding out in the hills," she informed him.

"I was just up there. Didn't come across his tracks though. Probably dug himself in somewhere pretty good."

"Why don't you just let them be, Brice? They're too dangerous. They could kill you."

"Not if I kill them first."

"Why does it have to come down to that? Why can't you just let them live and they'll let you live?"

"Cause this is what I do. Besides, they riled me up some. They're gonna get what's coming to them."

Ford realized that it was useless to try and convince him to give up hunting the outlaws. She was more afraid for him than she was for them. She had taken a liking to him that made her nervous for his well-being. Although she knew he was more than capable of killing the two outlaws, she knew Ashton and Keogh well enough to know that they were equally as capable of killing him. Symon bid Ford goodnight and went to the hotel for a room.

"There isn't gonna be any trouble tonight is there?" the clerk asked.

"If there is you're gonna need a new door."

"Why is that?"

"Cause that one will be full of holes," Symon bluntly told him.

"Oh," the clerk said as he handed Symon a key. "Enjoy your stay."

"You better hope so."

The night went by without incident. Nobody seemed to really care that Symon was back in town. Symon woke up with a beam of sun coming through the window shining down on his face. He had some breakfast then decided to check on Ashton. As he walked over to the jail he noticed a few people running in the streets like something was happening. Once he stepped inside he noticed the sheriff sitting at his desk.

"Mind if I check on Ashton?"

"Won't do you any good," the sheriff said.

"Why not?"

"Cause he ain't there."

"Where'd he go?"

"No idea. Looks like someone broke him out sometime during the night," the sheriff informed him.

"Where were you?"

"Asleep."

"And you didn't hear nothin'?" Symon wondered.

"I don't sleep here, Symon."

"Especially not with a prisoner here, right?"

"I can't be here 24 hours a day."

"How'd they break him out?"

"Looks like they found the key and unlocked the door," the sheriff said.

"Could it have been made any easier?" Symon said not surprised at what happened.

"Well, it is what it is. He's no longer here."

"You gonna get a posse after him?" Symon asked knowing what the answer would be.

"Nope. He's not my problem anymore. Not that it comes as any surprise to you.

"Can't say that it does."

"I guess that means you'll be leaving town soon," the sheriff hoped.

"Don't worry, I won't be back."

"Glad to hear it."

Just as Symon was about to leave the bearded cowboy walked in.

"Just coming for my reward money, Sheriff," the cowboy stated.

"Don't have it."

"Why not?"

"Cause you're not getting it."

"I brought him in, I deserve that money," the cowboy's voice raising. "That money's owed to me."

"Nothing's owed to you anymore. He ain't here no more so as far as I'm concerned he never was. They'll be no reward money."

"He's not here?"

"He escaped during the night."

"How can that be?"

"Don't know, just is. If you want that reward money you'll have to go find him and bring him to some other town. Just don't make it this one."

"I'll never come back here again."

"Seems to be the prevailing sentiment," Symon noted.

"Good. I don't want any of you around anyway," the sheriff said.

"You happen to know who broke him out?" Symon asked the sheriff.

"If I had to guess I'd say it was Ike Harper. He seems to be the only person who's disappeared from town today."

"Who's he?"

"You saw him last night."

"Where?"

"He's the one who killed the cowboy's two buddies," the sheriff explained.

"What can you tell me about him?"

"He's good friends with both Ashton and Keogh, though he don't usually ride with them. But he's a good gun as you can tell from last night."

"Is he wanted?" Symon wondered.

"Not to my knowledge."

"Much obliged."

"Forget it. Just don't come back."

Symon and the cowboy left the sheriff's office and contemplated their next move.

"You ridin' after him?" the cowboy asked.

"Yep."

"Mind if I tag along with ya?"

"Yep."

"Why? You can't bring him in by yourself."

"I've been doing this a long time and I never needed help from nobody. I reckon I won't need yours either."

"We could be partners. I can help you."

"You couldn't help me do a thing."

"Then you could help me. I'll do whatever you say. C'mon, what do you got to lose?"

"I've only had one partner in my life and he got killed. So it ain't what I got to lose...it's what you do. I don't take on partners anymore. I did it one time and it was one time too many."

"Well you can't stop me from looking for him myself," the cowboy told him.

"That's a fact, I can't stop you. But I'll give you some advice, you best stay out of my way or you'll end up like your friends."

"Is that a threat?"

"Nope. I don't make threats. I make promises. Just consider it some friendly advice."

"It's noted."

"You can also note this. You go after Ashton you're gonna get yourself killed. You're not a bounty hunter and you got no idea what you're doing, but if you're a mind to keep going that's up to you. But Ashton ain't no babe in the woods either, and he'll be waiting, most likely for me but he won't hesitate to kill you either," Symon said.

"I can handle myself. I got him once, I can get him again," the cowboy reasoned.

"Suit yourself."

Symon knew the cowboy was heading for a pine box. He only got Ashton before by surprise and with the help of two other men. He wouldn't have that luxury this time around if he went after him again. While Symon knew the man would meet a certain death, he didn't consider the idea of partnering up with him for even a second. The death of Conaghan was still too fresh in his mind. He couldn't envision taking a partner again. If he ever did, it'd have to be someone with experience. One of the reasons he was in the situation he is was because of Conaghan's lack of experience.

Symon grabbed his gear from the hotel and settled up at the main desk. He took his horse out of the stable and saddled him up before trotting out of town. As he rode past the final buildings he took a look back and noticed the cowboy getting on his horse and coming in the same direction. He had a feeling it wasn't the last time he'd be seeing him. Symon picked up a pair of horse tracks a little ways outside of town which must've been Ashton and Harper. The tracks indicated that they were headed for the hills. Maybe they were planning to meet up with Keogh. Symon rode for the hills and periodically looked back to see if the cowboy was still following. Though he didn't feel the cowboy was a threat to him, he was more of a nuisance that Symon could do without.

Symon rode pretty hard for the hills only slowing up periodically to give his horse a breather and to camp for the night. He could see a fire from a camp a little ways behind him which he figured was the cowboy trailing him. He smiled and shook his head in disbelief. Only a tenderfoot would light a fire making himself visible when he was trailing somebody. At this rate Symon figured the cowboy would be dead within a few days at most if he didn't pull himself together real quick. The next morning Symon rode at a regular pace as he entered the hills. He was very alert to his surroundings not knowing if the men he was pursuing would try to ambush him.

After a few hours he came across the remains of a camp that seemed pretty fresh. It couldn't have been more than a day old. Symon could tell that by the hoof prints in the dirt that there were at least two riders, possibly three. They were going further into the hills. Symon wasted no time in following. Some men that he pursued tried to cover up their tracks in hopes of throwing him off the trail. But these fellas didn't seem to care too much about that. They either didn't care that he was coming, or they wanted it to be obvious so they could bushwhack him at some point. Or it wasn't the men he was looking for. He'd already been thrown off the trail once before by the wrong man. And he still couldn't shake the uncomfortable feeling he had knowing the cowboy was following him. Now he knew how the men he tracked usually felt. The thought occurred to him that maybe he should slow down and let the cowboy catch up to him. Then if there was a trap being set up he wouldn't be the one walking into it. But that might mean giving up valuable time. Plus there was no guarantee that he'd actually find them since he wasn't experienced at this line of work. Symon quickly decided to keep on going the way things were and just hope that the cowboy didn't wind up getting in his way.

Chapter 7

Symon stopped his horse at the edge of a stream as he let it drink some water. He dismounted and surveyed the area around him. He walked a little ways holding the reins of the horse checking the ground for fresh hoof prints embedded in the dirt. After a few minutes of searching he found the tracks of two horses that looked to be crossing the stream. Symon mounted his horse and rode through the stream, the horse splashing water around him. Upon reaching dry land Symon got off his horse once again and checked the tracks. He was a little surprised by what he saw though. Instead of picking up the two sets of tracks from the other side of the stream he was now seeing an extra one. There were three horses there. Kneeling on one knee Symon took his hat off with his arm resting on his other knee looking out into the distance thinking about the situation. He figured that Ashton and Harper had met up with Keogh right at this spot. He followed the tracks which didn't stray too far from the stream.

Symon followed the three down the stream for quite a spell. After about an hour or so the tracks disappeared, which only meant one thing, they crossed the stream again. Symon rode to the other side again and sure enough picked them up. It looked like they were doubling back. He assumed they were either trying to take him on from behind or they decided to wait for him not realizing he was as close behind as he was. Symon cautiously rode along waiting for some sign of trouble. He was ready for it. It wouldn't take very long for him to find it though. Within the hour he heard shooting. Sounded like a big conflict as the shots were ringing out in rapid succession for a few minutes. Thinking that it may have been the outlaws he was looking for Symon hastily rode towards the booming shots. As he approached the area he noticed smoke coming from a clump of trees. His head snapped to attention, turning in every direction, as a few more shots rang out. He noticed more smoke rising in the air above a downed tree. Symon approached the area carefully as he took out his rifle after dismounting his horse tying it to a nearby tree.

"What happened to Symon, he leave ya all alone to fend for yourself?" one of the men hollered from the clump of trees.

"He's around," a man shouted back from behind the downed tree.

Symon could tell it was the bearded cowboy who was pinned down behind the tree. He couldn't make out who was among the clump of trees but was assuming, or expecting, it to be the men he was hunting. Symon decided to wait a few more minutes before making his presence known. If it was the outlaws he was going to try and wait for them to give him a good target to shoot at. The men exchanged a few more rounds without either really doing much of anything except wasting ammunition.

"Throw down your gun and give your word you won't hunt us no more and we'll let you go on your way," one of them yelled.

"How do I know I can trust ya?"

"Guess there's no way of tellin' for sure. You'll just have to take our word for it."

"That don't sound too appealing."

Symon positioned himself a little behind the cowboy's spot. He wanted to try and move somewhere between the cowboy and the outlaws but didn't think he could without being seen. There were a lot of trees around but not much else to hide his movements and most of the trees were spaced out from each other. He had a big advantage at the moment since they didn't know that he was there and he didn't want to lose it without getting at least one shot in. The cowboy suddenly jumped up and tried sprinting to another spot. About midway there he was stopped and stumbled to the ground from one of the barrage of bullets levied his way. The three men who shot him emerged from their position to check on their fallen victim. The cowboy noticed the men approaching and tried crawling to reach his revolver which flew out of his hand when the bullet entered his leg. Symon knew he'd have to finally intervene. He could now make out their faces and he couldn't have asked for anything better. He had clear shots at the outlaws. As the men raised their guns to finish off the wounded cowboy Symon announced his presence under a hail of gunfire. He wounded Keogh in the thigh and hit Harper in the wrist. Harper and Ashton scurried back among the trees and Keogh dropped behind the downed tree in excruciating pain from the bullet that was entrenched in his leg. The cowboy crawled over to his gun and picked it up as he made it behind a thick tree sitting up against it.

"Who is that?" Keogh asked, pain tainting his voice slightly.

"Think you already know the answer to that question," Symon replied.

"Brice Symon," Keogh shouted. "You shot me in the leg you bastard."

"Bad shootin'. I was aiming for your chest."

"Should've killed me when you had the chance."

"I still intend to."

"I think you'll end up being disappointed."

"Not likely," Symon said to himself.

Symon fired a couple shots at Keogh before taking cover from some shots fired by Ashton and Harper.

"You're outnumbered Symon! We can keep firing shots at each other all day if you want but it ain't gonna change nothin'," Ashton screamed.

"So why don't you just throw your guns down and give it up. Make it easier on everybody," Symon replied.

"Not quite what I had in mind."

"Maybe not. But it's what I got in mind."

"You can't get all three of us."

"Don't bet on it."

"What's it gonna take for you to go away Symon?" Keogh asked.

"You being silent and cold."

"I thought so. Not very hospitable of you."

"No, I reckon it ain't. But it is what it is."

Ashton fired a few rounds at Symon to keep him at bay while Harper broke out from the clump of trees and made it to a nearby tree. Harper had a pretty clear sight of the bearded cowboy from his position. He was unable to raise his hand with his wounded wrist so he tried to steady the gun gripping it with his left hand pressing it firmly against the tree. He fired one shot that went clean through the cowboy's shoulder. The cowboy raised to his feet to return fire but was dropped by another bullet that lodged into his stomach. Harper left himself a little vulnerable with the second shot as he had to position himself in a way that left part of him exposed. Symon noticed and let a few shots rip from the barrel of his rifle. One bullet split some bark off the tree but the second shot grazed the cheek of Harper ripping the flesh off his face. Harper screamed in agony lying on the ground. After a few moments he composed himself and got up still in a lot of pain.

"You alright, Ike?" Ashton yelled over.

"I'm still breathing. He's mine. I want him," Harper told him becoming angrier with each passing moment.

"Just sit tight. Don't do anything hasty."

Harper was too angry to listen to anything reasonable though. He was determined to kill Symon himself. He moved out from the tree to get closer to him. Symon noticed him running and popped up from his spot and fired a shot that missed Harper. Symon fired again and hit Harper in the right bicep that made him stumble and fall to both knees. Just as Harper gained his feet again Symon let another shot fly from rifle hitting Harper square in the chest. Harper fell to his knees again dropping his pistol and holding his chest with both hands. Symon took aim and fired again hitting Harper in the chest once more instantly taking the last breath of life he had left in him.

"Ike!" Ashton shouted.

"Ain't no use, Ashton. He's gone."

"You don't sound so happy about it."

"Well there ain't no price on his head that I know of. He cost me a few bullets though," Symon explained as he reloaded his rifle.

"Shame."

"Looks like your odds are decreasing."

"How you figure?" Ashton wondered.

"Lost your man."

"You lost one, we lost one. Sounds like an even swap. You're still out-numbered."

"By my count there's only two of you. Seems to me like you got the short end of the stick," Symon said.

"You're a funny man."

"Not as funny as you. Keogh's gonna need some doctorin' soon or else it's just gonna be me and you. Then you'll really be in a pickle."

"Symon," the cowboy shouted out.

"Just sit tight," Symon answered.

"Help me."

"Not much I can do for you right now."

"I think I'm dying."

"Well if you are, I'm afraid there ain't much I can do for ya."

"You need to help me," the cowboy pined.

"If you don't shut up and stop your bellyaching I'll finish you off my-self. Now sit still."

"He's dying, Symon. If you don't get him to a doctor soon he's gonna die," Ashton offered.

"Makes no difference to me. He ain't no kin or friend of mine."

"He's helping you out ain't he?"

"Can't say that he is. Didn't ask for his help, didn't ask for him to tag along, didn't ask for a damn thing from him. Whether he lives or dies is of no consequence to me."

"That almost sounds like me talkin'. Maybe we're rubbin' off on ya."

"Not likely."

"Maybe you could throw in with us."

"Hell would freeze over first."

Silence took over for the next few minutes as they all contemplated what the best course of action would be. Keogh had been pretty quiet for the last few minutes as he tried to stop his leg from bleeding. It was a pretty clean wound as the bullet passed straight through his leg without hitting any arteries but he was still in a little bit of discomfort.

"Awful quiet down there Keogh, doing OK?" Symon sarcastically asked.

"Don't you worry 'bout me Symon. I'll live to see you buried."

None of the men seemed to have any kind of advantage with their position that would make it easy to end the conflict. Each of them had dug in to their spots and were pretty comfortable in their respective positions. Harper and the cowboy had taken chances to get to what they thought were better spots and it cost both of them dearly. The other three were not about to make the same mistakes. None of them were about to make the first move that would lead to any further action but they were each waiting for someone else to try something. After a half hour of waiting each other out it occurred to Symon that he'd have to come up with a plan to get things started. He had an idea that he hoped would make the outlaws turn on each other to save their own hide and split the two up.

"Hear me Ashton?" Symon asked.

"Unfortunately so."

"It would seem that we're at a stalemate."

"Looks that way don't it?"

"Have a proposition for ya."

"I'm listenin'," Ashton replied.

"What? Ain't got nothin' for me Symon?" Keogh wondered.

"Not at the moment. I'll get around to you though."

"Let him talk Sloan," Ashton told him. "What ya got in mind?"

"I'm willing to let you ride out of here right now."

"What's the catch?"

"No catch. You ride out of here. You and you alone. I take Keogh."

"I don't much care for that deal."

"Least that way you'll get somewhat of a chance. Make no mistake I'm not letting you off the hook. I'll let you go today but I'll be back. You won't be seeing the last of me. I'll be coming after you again. Most likely get a week or so head start on me. You couldn't ask for a better chance than that."

"Don't listen to him, Trist," Keogh shouted. "He's just trying to split us up. He knows he can't take the both of us right now. Just hold your ground."

"Easy for him to say, Ashton. With that hole in his leg he needs you more than you need him. I could leave right now but with him slowing you up I'd get you in a day or so anyway. Do the smart thing for once."

"Trist, I swear if you take off I'll hunt you down and kill you myself."

There was no answer from Ashton which was unusual as he almost always had something to say. He was deeply considering Symon's offer.

"Say something Trist," Keogh yelled over.

"I'm thinkin'."

"C'mon Ashton, you're not as dumb as he is, are you?" Symon asked.

"Shut up, Symon," Keogh shouted.

"What do you think Keogh would do if the situation was reversed? You think he'd hesitate leaving you? I guarantee he would've left about ten minutes ago."

"How much time you giving me?" Ashton wondered.

"As much time as it takes me to bring Keogh in. Then I'll be lookin' for ya."

Ashton considered the offer for a few more minutes before deciding what to do.

"So what's it gonna be Ashton?" Symon asked, interrupting the silence.

"It's a deal."

"I swear I'm gonna kill you Trist. After I got you free from him you're gonna turn on me like this? I give you my word you're a dead man," Keogh shouted angrily.

"I'm much obliged to you for that Sloan, I truly am, but a man's gotta look after his self in times like these. I wish you good luck partner."

"For your sake you better hope Symon shoots me or they hang me cause if they don't you're gonna die the slowest most miserable death imaginable."

"Alright Symon, I'm backing away and riding out," Ashton informed him.

Symon watched as Ashton rode his horse away from the area. He took note of the direction he was heading so he could pick up his trail later.

"You're making one big mistake Symon," Keogh shouted.

"How you figure?"

"You're thinkin' I'm just gonna roll over and let you take me in. I ain't on my deathbed. I may be shot but it ain't lethal yet. I'm still as dangerous as you are."

"That may be so but I don't reckon you'll be movin' too swiftly. You might be able to still shoot but you ain't never gonna make it to a horse."

"Looks like that means we're stalemated too, don't it?" Keogh stated.

"Not hardly. I can wait here as long as it takes. With that hole in your leg, I reckon you can't afford to do the same. Sooner or later you gotta make a move."

Keogh knew Symon was speaking the truth. He was gonna need a doctor eventually, preferably sooner rather than later. But he didn't know how he was gonna get himself out of the situation he found himself in.

"You must be stewin' something pretty bad knowing that Ashton took off and left ya. Especially after you done what you did for hm. Must hurt pretty bad knowing how ungrateful he is you sticking your neck out for him but him not doing the same," Symon told him.

"He'll get his."

"That's true, but unfortunately for you, it won't be from your hands, it'll be from mine."

"I think that's still yet to be determined," Keogh stated. "Hey, I got a deal for you Symon."

"What's that?"

"How bout I let you ride off right now and I won't kill you today. What do you think of that?" Keogh said laughing.

"I think I'll pass on that one."

"Your funeral."

"So where you think Ashton's going?" Symon asked.

"Probably to Denton."

"Why so?"

"He's got a girl there."

"He's got another girl? What about Ford?" Symon wondered.

"What, you think he only has one? If you think he's the kind of guy who'd only love one woman you're crazy."

"She seemed like a decent enough woman. Pretty enough anyway."

"The looks to make most women jealous and tougher than some men I know of," Keogh replied.

"Sounds like the ideal woman."

"Would be for most. Ashton ain't the kind to ever settle down though. Besides, you met him, you know he's got a few screws loose."

"That's a fact," Symon said. "Ready to give yourself up yet?"

"I don't give up."

"Darn shame for ya."

"Even if I did, I thought you didn't take prisoners?" the outlaw asked.

"I don't. I'd prefer you stick your head out so I could blow it off."

"Why don't you let me get a shot off at yours. Maybe I'll improve your looks."

"All your yappin' is making me lose time on Ashton," Symon informed him.

"Well then why don't you go grab him. I'll wait here for you. Give you my word."

"I'd rather just bury you so I can get on my way. Taking you to town would seem to be more hassle than it's worth don't you think?"

Keogh quickly rolled over propping his gun on the fallen tree and fired off a couple rounds in Symon's direction. Symon returned fire with a few shots of his own. It was unlikely that either one was gonna do any damage from their current position. In a swift moment Symon sprinted over to the tree next to him. Keogh didn't notice that he had changed positions.

"I seen one arm men shoot better than you," Keogh yelled out.

Symon didn't reply thinking Keogh would start sweating it out a little more if he wasn't sure where Symon was. He'd start panicking and make a mistake.

"Symon?"

There was still no reply. Keogh peeked up slightly so his eyes were just barely able to see over the tree. He didn't see any movement anywhere. His nerves were starting to get to him not knowing where Symon was.

"Why don't you show your face? Getting a little scared?" Keogh asked hoping for an answer.

He still didn't get one.

"Answer me Symon!"

Symon quickly brought his rifle into shooting position and fired a shot that hit the tree that was covering Keogh right near his eyes kicking up a piece of it with some dust getting into Keogh's eyes. Symon noticed he was temporarily blinded and ran closer to him before he was able to recover. Keogh wiped his eyes and was able to notice Symon moving closer although not clearly. Keogh fired a shot in Symon's direction that wasn't really that close. Symon kept moving forward as Keogh fired again that was much closer to his target. Symon dove near another tree rolled over onto his stomach and fired his rifle not hitting anything.

"Symon, how bout we do this like men?"

"How you figure?" Symon responded.

"Instead of each of us rolling around in the dirt and hiding behind trees what do you say we face each other and look each other in the eye?"

"You want a gunfight?"

"I don't suspect either one of us is gonna get the upper hand any other way. Neither of us is gonna do nothin' to take any chances. We could be here all day at this rate. Let's get this over with."

"Only problem with that is that I ain't in no hurry," Symon noted.

"You got a yellow streak runnin' down your back?" Keogh asked.

"I've faced better men than you. You couldn't take me on my worst day."

"Prove it."

"I don't need to prove it especially with that leg of yours. You can bleed to death for all I care. I don't need to do a thing."

"That'd be true if it was still bleeding. But it ain't so you don't need to worry 'bout that."

Symon wasn't quite sure that he believed his leg stopped bleeding. He thought Keogh might've just been bluffing about it. He didn't feel the need to engage in a gunfight when he already had the upper hand. It would've been a fool's play. Only a desperate man would take that offer. And nobody would ever mistake Brice Symon as being desperate or a fool.

"So what do you say, Symon?"

"I'll pass."

Keogh knew Symon had the upperhand as things were but it was worth a try. His leg was still bleeding though not badly. But he still needed to have it looked at soon. He didn't have anything else to even things out so he'd have to wait till Symon made his move. Symon could tell Keogh was getting overanxious or else he wouldn't have tried for a gunfight. If he was in a good spot a man like that wouldn't try to be bargaining for an even fight. He'd be looking for every advantage he could get. Symon knew it was time to make his move.

Chapter 8

Symon felt it was the right time to end the stand-off. He fired a shot at Keogh to make him take cover and then made a run for his position. After taking a few seconds to collect himself Keogh could hear Symon moving positions by the sounds of the leaves and twigs he was running on. He quickly propped himself up in time to see Symon almost on top of him. Keogh hurriedly fired a shot that missed Symon as he dove over the fallen tree. As Symon hit the ground he rolled over to his stomach and positioned his rifle to fire a shot. Keogh turned around to face his foe but was not as quick as Symon. Symon fired his rifle hitting Keogh in the right forearm causing him to drop his revolver.

"You did it again," Keogh yelled out in pain, holding his arm.

"Purely unintentional."

"You did it deliberately."

"Not likely. I'd much rather take you back draped over a saddle instead of you sitting on top of one," Symon informed him.

Keogh gave thought to making a play for his gun on the ground. Symon saw his eyes look in that direction and could tell he had thoughts about trying for it. Symon continued walking in his direction as Keogh clutched his arm.

"As much as I'd love to plug you where you stand I wouldn't if I was you," Symon told him.

"What's that?"

"I can see it in your eyes. You're wondering whether you have enough time to grab that gun and kill me before I have time to get another shot off."

"Could be."

"You don't," Symon said matter of factly.

Keogh looked at the rifle Symon was carrying by his side and determined that the bounty hunter was right. He wasn't going to chance something when the odds were clearly not in his favor. Symon was very
proficient with that rifle and would've killed him before he even picked his
gun up. He figured he would still have a couple more chances to escape
before his time was up. Symon tied Keogh to a tree before gathering up the
horses. As he was about to put Keogh up on his horse he heard a groan.
The cowboy was still alive, though barely. Symon walked over to him
pulling Keogh along with him. Symon knelt down to check on the badly
injured man. He moved the cowboy's hands away from his stomach to
check on his wound and winced once he saw how bad it was.

"Don't leave me," the cowboy pleaded.

Symon ran his hand over his forehead and his eyes thinking about what
he should do. He knew the cowboy's days were most likely numbered. He
didn't have much of a chance of surviving riding back to town.

"He's finished Symon, leave him," Keogh stated.

The cowboy said something that was so low Symon couldn't make it
out. He was breathing heavy and his energy to speak was evaporating
quickly. Symon moved closer to him and asked him to say it again.

"I can still ride," the cowboy said breathing heavily still.

"He'll be dead in a few hours and you know it. Why bother?" Keogh
said.

"Man should have a chance. Every man deserves at least that much."

"Ah, you're gettin' all preachy. Dead is dead. And that fella's dead. Ain't
no way around that."

Symon knew he was speaking the truth as much as he hated to admit it
to himself. The cowboy had as bad a gut-shot wound as he could ever recall
seeing before. But even though he didn't think he'd make it too much
longer, he was still breathing, and he wasn't sure he could just leave a
wounded man behind no matter what his chances were. He would undoubtedly slow him up even further. Bringing Keogh back alive was going to slow

him up enough as he was sure he'd have a few tricks up his sleeve. But he wouldn't be able to ride with any kind of haste if he had to worry about bringing back a badly wounded man also. Symon stood up and grabbed Keogh and led him to their horses. He put Keogh on his horse and was ready to mount his when he looked back at the cowboy lying on the ground. With his hands on his saddle he buried his head into his horse. He looked over again and couldn't believe what he was seeing. He squinted and looked even more intently on the object. He was seeing an image of his wife standing in front of the wounded man. Although he had seen her in dreams and flashbacks it was the first time he'd ever seen her standing before him like this.

"Do the right thing Brice," she told him.

Symon took his eyes off her only for a second before looking back but she was gone. He looked around as if he was waiting for her to appear somewhere else.

"Get off your horse," Symon told Keogh.

"Why?"

"Cause you're gonna give me a hand."

"Why should I?"

Symon pulled his pistol and pointed it at Keogh.

"I got six reasons right here why you should."

"And good reasons they are," Keogh stated as he got off his horse.

Symon grabbed another horse and got it ready. Then he and Keogh went over to the cowboy and started to gently pick him up.

"You understand I'll do what I can for ya, but I can't do much," Symon told him.

"Just get me to town."

"You gonna be able to stay on your horse?" Symon asked.

"If not you just tie me to it."

Symon and Keogh walked him over to his horse and helped him mount up. Once on top the cowboy rocked his head back and looked straight up almost as if he was gonna fall backwards but somehow managed to balance himself and stay on.

"I think you're makin' a mistake with this one," Keogh told him.

"I've made 'em before. Besides, what's it to you?"

"Nothin'. Nothin' at all. I was just sayin' is all."

"Next time say it to yourself."

They started riding for the nearest town which was Baxtor Springs. It was probably a two day ride. It was possible to make it in one but not with the men Symon was riding with to slow him up. They rode at a pretty slow pace for the first couple of hours. As they were riding along Symon suddenly heard a thump. He looked just behind him and saw that the cowboy had fallen off his horse.

"Slow it up Keogh," Symon told him.

The men halted their horses as Symon dismounted to check on the cowboy.

"He dead yet?" Keogh wondered.

"Not yet."

Symon helped him back up and put him back on his horse.

"Gonna make it?" Symon asked him again.

"I'll make it."

"Since when did you start going all soft?" Keogh asked.

"Why don't you shut your mouth for once?" Symon replied.

"I'm just askin'."

Symon put the cowboy's hands on the horn of his saddle and gripped them tight.

"You hold on tight now, hear?" Symon told him.

The cowboy just slightly nodded his head. Symon wasn't sure if he had much time left though he was surprised he made it as far as he did. He was tougher than he had given him credit for.

"Never would have taken you for a compassionate man," Keogh said.

"I ain't much."

They rode for another hour before hearing that thud sound when a body hits the ground. The men looked back and noticed that the cowboy had fallen off his horse again. Symon looked over at Keogh.

"I know, I know, slow it up," stated Keogh.

Symon got off his horse again to check on him. It was no use trying to get him back on a horse this time though. He wasn't breathing anymore. He finally succumbed to his wounds though he fought it off for as long as he could.

"What's a matter, Symon?" Keogh shouted.

"Ain't gonna have to worry about him no more," Symon told him.

"He's a goner?"

"He's gone."

"Well it's about time. I was beginnin' to think the old coot was never gonna die."

Symon picked the cowboy up and laid him across the saddle of his horse and tied him to it to make sure he didn't fall off again. Symon and Keogh then picked up the pace without having to worry about the straggler.

"What do you seem so bent out of shape for that fella for?" Keogh asked.

"I ain't really."

"Coulda fooled me with you carin' for him like you done. I thought you wasn't friends."

"We weren't."

"Then why go through all this? You knew he was gonna die as well as I did. Why not just leave him behind?" Keogh wondered.

"I dunno really. Just didn't seem like the right thing to do."

"Well maybe it's just me then. I reckon I ain't never figured out the right thing to do about much of anything. I usually do the wrong thing."

"I reckon so."

"Where we heading anyway?"

"Baxtor Springs."

"Why there?"

"Cause that's the closest town. I also know the sheriff there. It ain't gonna be like back in Kingman."

"No, I guess not. That was a sweet little setup we had going on there though."

"Can't argue with that."

They continued riding through nightfall not stopping for anything other than letting the horses drink some water and rest a little bit.

"When we making camp?" Keogh wanted to know.

"We're not."

"What do you mean?"

"I mean we're not stopping," Symon informed him.

"We can make Baxtor Springs before morning. I ain't taking no chances with you trying something in the middle of the night while I'm sleeping."

"With all we been through I feel a might ashamed that you still don't trust me."

"You and Ashton really like hearing yourselves talk don't ya?"

"Sometimes that's all ya got to listen to."

"Ever try just listening to the silence?" Symon asked.

"What good would that do? You can't hear silence," Keogh replied.

Symon just shook his head in amusement. They kept on riding and arrived at Baxtor Springs a few hours before sunrise. The town was eerily quiet which was not to be unexpected at that time of the night. Symon stopped the horses in front of the sheriff's office and walked Keogh inside. Symon went over to the desk and lit a lamp. He looked around then went into the back part of the jail in search of someone but he had no luck.

"Maybe we should try the next town," Keogh stated.

"Shut up."

Symon walked out into the street pulling Keogh along with him. They went to the hotel and Symon noticed the desk clerk hunched over sleeping in a chair. He rang the bell a few times before the clerk finally woke up and stumbled to the desk to wait on the gentlemen.

"What can I do for you gents?"

"First thing would be a room," Symon said.

"One for each of you?"

"Just me."

"What about you, sir?" the clerk asked Keogh.

"He'll be making other arrangements," Symon told him.

"Well alright. Your room is number 17. It'll be upstairs to your left," the clerk said as he handed Symon a key. "Anything else I can do for you?"

"Yeah, you can fetch the sheriff."

"What for?"

"Tell him I have a present for him."

"Couldn't it wait till morning?"

"Now," Symon said sternly.

"Well where should I have him meet you?"

"I'll be waiting in his office."

"Who should I say is calling?"

"The tooth fairy."

Symon and Keogh walked back over to the jail and sat down in the office and waited for the sheriff to come. About ten minutes later the sheriff came walking in. He looked both men over sizing up the situation. He then walked up to Symon who was sitting at his desk.

"I don't like anyone sitting at my desk," the sheriff told him.

"Maybe if you were doing your job and been here then I wouldn't have been able to sit in this rackety old chair," Symon shot back.

"Mister, you keep talkin' like that and you better be reachin' for those guns soon."

"Why, you couldn't hit a tree if you were standing in a forest."

Keogh couldn't believe his luck. He thought if the two of them shot it out that maybe they'd kill each other and he'd be able to go on his way.

"Who's your friend?" the sheriff asked looking in Keogh's direction.

"No friend of mine."

"You got two choices. You can either get up or I'll beat you so bad you won't recognize yourself."

"Mighty big talk for a fat man."

The sheriff finally smiled at Symon's insults. Symon got up and walked over to him and stuck his hand out. The sheriff let a smile overtake his face and the two men shook hands.

"What do you mean fat?" the sheriff asked.

"Look like you put on a few pounds since I seen you last," Symon explained.

"Only a couple."

"Uh huh."

"So how you doin'?"

"Not too bad."

"Who's this guy?" the sheriff wanted to know.

"Sloan Keogh."

"Oh yeah? Would've recognized him better if I wasn't half asleep."

"Sorry Paul."

"Ah, it's no big deal. You get kinda used to it after a while."

"Lock him up for me?"

"No problem," the sheriff told him as he grabbed the keys for the cells and locked Keogh up.

The two men walked outside when the sheriff noticed a man laying across a horse.

"What's this?"

"Died a few hours ago."

"He wanted for anything?" the sheriff asked.

"Nope, 'fraid not."

"Well what happened?"

"Just a casualty of the situation."

"Friend of yours?"

"No, he just tried to be something he wasn't," Symon explained.

"Well, leave him here and I'll take care of him. So what happened?"

"I'd like to talk to you more, Paul, but I'm a little tired. I want to get my horse settled and get some sleep. What do you say we pick it up later?" Symon offered.

"Won't get any arguments from me on that one," the sheriff agreed.

The sheriff led the cowboy away as Symon took his horse to the livery stable. After Symon got his horse settled he went back to the hotel. The clerk was there waiting for Symon to return.

"Everything OK with the sheriff?" the clerk nosily wondered.

"Yep."

"Anything else I can get you?"

"Nope."

"What happened to your friend?"

"He made other sleeping arrangements."

"But this is the only hotel in town."

"I know," Symon replied as he walked up the stairs to his room. "Oh, there is one more thing you can do for me."

"Yes sir?"

"Make sure nobody bothers me."

"Yes sir."

Symon was finally able to lay his tired body down on the bed and instantly fell asleep. He woke up late in the morning hearing a few birds chirping. He got up and stretched a bit before walking to the window and looking out. He'd been there before and some people in town already knew who he was. Although this was the first time he actually stayed overnight. He'd passed through two previous times not spending much time there though. Symon got himself ready and left his room before walking down to the hotel lobby.

"Enjoy your night?" the clerk asked.

"Very quiet," Symon replied as he walked out into the street.

He went over to the sheriff's office to check on Keogh. The sheriff wasn't around so Symon went into the back room where Keogh was staying.

"Not like staying in Kingman is it?" Symon asked.

"Not at all."

"Need anything?"

"A gun would be nice."

"So you don't need anything," Symon concluded.

"Tell me about this sheriff."

"Why?"

"Just curious. I like to know about the men I'm up against."

"His name's Paul Ellis. Been the sheriff here for a few years now I guess. He's a good man."

"I'll be the judge of that."

"He's a pretty sharp guy, he can shoot pretty well, and he's got a lot of guts. You're no match for him if you're planning on trying something," Symon informed him.

"Don't sound promising does it?"

Symon heard someone entering the office and checked to see who it was and saw it was Ellis.

"Howdy Brice," Ellis greeted.

"Paul," Symon responded.

"Should have your bounty money a little later on in the day."

"Suits me fine."

"So what happened out there?" Ellis wondered.

"I'd like to talk about it but I ain't ate breakfast yet," Symon said.

"Well how bout we talk while eating?"

"Sounds good to me."

Ellis and Symon left and went to the town restaurant. They had some eggs, bacon, and coffee and started talking about what they'd been up to.

"So what are you planning now that you brought Keogh in?" Ellis asked.

"His partner's still out there."

"Trist Ashton?"

"That's right."

"Know where he's at?"

"Have a pretty good idea. Had him once already but he escaped out of Kingman."

"Escaped? You brought him back alive? That reminds me, you brought Keogh back alive too. What's going on? That's not like you," Ellis said.

"Don't remind me. I had a few other circumstances get in my way."

"Like the fella we buried earlier?"

"Well, he's one of them."

"Who is he?"

"Can't say I ever did know his name. Far as I know he's just a drifter who thought he'd give bounty hunting a try. Came across the wrong men."

"That it?"

"Took on a youngster a little ways back who asked and convinced me to teach him the trade. He was a kid by the name of Conaghan. He got the drop on one of 'em and we wound up trying to take him back till Keogh came along and they escaped. They shot and killed him. Now it's personal. I didn't do the boy right. I feel like I could've done more to help him. Maybe he'd still be livin'."

"Can't let it eat at you Brice. You've already got enough things eating away at you. Things gotten any better with that?" Ellis wondered.

"I still miss them. I don't think I'll ever forget."

"Maybe you just need to settle down in one spot again. Too much time on your hands out there hunting. Out there all alone makes a man think too much."

"Could be, but I don't think I'd be able to do anything else again. I'm too far gone now."

"You talk like you're dying."

"Some days it seems like I am," Symon revealed.

After a few minutes of silence and both men eating Symon tried to get the conversation on a lighter note.

"So what about you? Find a woman yet willing to put up with you?"

"Not yet. Still got a lotta time though," Ellis said with a smile.

They finished eating and decided to talk a walk around the town.

"So where's your deputy? I haven't seen him since I been here," Symon asked.

"He was killed a few months back."

"What happened?"

"A bunch of cowboys came riding in one night. Got themselves all liquored up and started making trouble. When he got there to get them to quiet down they just pulled their weapons and started shootin'. Killed him instantly. Never had a chance," Ellis remembered.

"Darn shame. So you haven't hired anybody else yet?"

"Not yet. The men I'd like to have aren't interested and the ones who are I don't want."

They talked about the town for a little while before going on their separate ways. They agreed to meet later in the afternoon when the reward money would be available. Until then Symon figured he would just try to relax for most of the day. He actually looked forward to it since he didn't get to do it too often. He found an unoccupied chair by the barber shop that he decided to fill. He just sat there for a couple hours watching the town go about its normal, daily routine.

Chapter 9

After spending most of the day sitting in front of the barber shop and playing solitaire by himself in the saloon Symon figured he'd given Ellis enough time to get the money he had coming. Just as he was about to finish up with the cards a man sat came up to his table.

"Mind if I talk to you for a bit?" the man asked while sitting down.

"Looks like you already are," Symon replied, a little annoyed that the man took it upon himself to sit down without being invited.

"You're Brice Symon right?" the well dressed man asked.

"Yep. Who wants to know?"

"The name's Horatio Mendenthal."

"What do you want?"

"You like to get right to the point don't you, Mister Symon?"

"Mostly."

"Well I'm the owner of the establishment you're sitting in."

"And?"

"Well there's several people here in town who would like you to get Sloan Keogh out of jail," the wealthy elderly man revealed.

"Get him out? What do you mean, get him out, I just put him in."

"Well as I mentioned there are several individuals in town who would like to see him somewhere else."

"So what's it got to do with me?"

"Well you brought him in."

"That don't mean nothin'. I can't get him out now. He's in the hands of the law."

"But for how long?" Mendenthal asked.

"You sure don't like getting to the point do you? I've got to admit you're one of the most confusing men I've ever had the pleasure or displeasure of conversating with. I don't understand a thing you're implying."

"We all know he has a partner and friends. The longer he stays in that jail there's bound to be trouble here eventually. They may be on their way here already."

"I doubt that."

"How can you be sure?"

"I chased his partner away yesterday."

"So he's already in the area then?"

"He don't know he's here."

"How do you know?"

"Cause I know when I'm being followed and nobody followed me here."

"I'm looking out for the well-being of this town. Please take him somewhere else."

"Can't do that. Besides, you've got as good a sheriff here as any town I've come across."

"Oh I'm not saying anything bad against Sheriff Ellis. He's a good man. But he's only one man. What if six or seven of his men ride in? If Keogh's men come through here he'll be severely outnumbered."

"So what is it that you want from me?" Symon asked.

"To get Keogh out of this town," Mendenthal stated.

"And just how do you want me to accomplish that?"

"You'll figure out a way."

"And just where is it that you want me to take him?"

"Doesn't matter. Anywhere but here."

"So you don't care if anybody dies or another town gets shot up, as long as it isn't this one?" Symon asked with a touch of anger in his voice.

"It would be unfortunate but they're not my problem. All I can do is look out for the town I'm in."

"So why should I help you? I got no stake in this town. I couldn't care less what happens to any of ya."

"You wouldn't care if this town was shot full of holes or burned by a bunch of outlaws?"

"I think you're overreacting a little bit," Symon said with an amusing smile.

"I'm not the only one in town who doesn't like the fact that you brought him here."

Symon grabbed his hat that was on the table and put it on after standing up. He pushed his chair away giving Mendenthal a final glance.

"That's tough," Symon told him as he walked through the saloon doors.

Symon walked over to Ellis' office and saw the sheriff sitting at his desk.

"My money come through yet?" Symon asked.

"Not yet. You're really anxious aren't you?"

"Just wanna be on my way. Each hour that passes is another hour that Ashton is slipping away from me. Plus I'd like to get out of this town as soon as possible," he said as he looked out the window.

"Why? Got trouble?"

"No, but you will."

"What do you mean?" the sheriff quizzed.

"I just had a visit from a Mendenthal. I think that was his name."

"Horatio Mendenthal. He owns the saloon. One of the more influential citizens in town."

"Yeah, I kinda gathered that."

"What's going on?"

"He wanted me to get Keogh out of here."

"He what?!"

"He said that the town's a little afraid that Ashton and his gang are gonna come bust him out of jail and make the town a little holy."

"What do you think?"

"It's a lot of nonsense. There's nothing left of their gang. They've all been killed except for Ashton and Keogh. And Ashton is most likely on his way to Denton. So that means that nobody's coming here to bust him out of jail," Symon said pointing at the cell.

"Well that's good to know."

"Too bad they don't believe it," Symon said as he nodded to a crowd gathering in front of the saloon.

There was no doubt they were starting to get worked up about Keogh being in their jail. Ellis didn't take long to decide he needed to act quickly. He immediately left to talk to the gathering group of townsfolk. Symon watched from the window as he saw Ellis trying to talk sense to the men. Some of the men seemed to be getting pretty animated in trying to get their point across. After a few more minutes Ellis came walking back to the office.

"What's the verdict?" Symon curiously asked.

"Didn't do a bit of good," Ellis responded tossing his hat on the desk.

"Had a feeling it wouldn't."

"Well it's even worse than I hoped."

"How's that?"

"Not only did I not succeed in telling them to go away, I got the feeling that they may try to set Keogh free themselves. I believe there was a mention or two in regards to a rope as well."

"Lynchin'?"

"Yeah."

"Fools. If he still had a gang and they came to bust him loose and saw him hanged what do you think they'd do then? Just turn around and ride out? They'd definitely shoot the town up after that."

"You know it and I know it, but they don't. And I don't think they can be convinced," Ellis said.

"Don't envy you here, Paul. You got a powderkeg on your hands."

"I know it. Do me a favor Brice?"

"You know I'll do what I can for you."

"Let me deputize you."

"What?!"

"Just for a day or two."

"I think you went and lost your head. Someone club you over the head when you went out there?" Symon quipped.

"If they turn into a mob I don't think I can hold him on my own."

"Well I ain't no lawman."

"They know your reputation. Just you being here with me might deter them."

"I think you've gone plum crazy."

"You haven't gotten your reward money yet. If they bust him loose I have no obligation to pay you."

"I brung him in, if you can't hold him that's your problem, not mine," Symon animatedly said, pointing at Ellis before pointing back at himself with his thumb.

"To me it'd be like he was never even here."

"Now that's playing dirty Paul."

"It is what it is," Ellis said with a shrug. "Besides, it's in your best interests to help me."

"How you figure that?"

"If they let him go you'll just have to capture him all over again."

"Oh, there won't be no capture. If he gets out of that cell I'll bring him back colder than a December morning and that's a promise."

"What if they lynch him?"

"Then I want my money."

"You can't be in favor of that. No man deserves to be lynched."

"I don't know about that. I can think of quite a few men who deserve to be swinging from the end of a rope."

"Legally, yes. But not lynching."

"Oh what's the difference. A rope is a rope and dead is dead."

"So you're not gonna help me then?"

Symon looked away towards the floor taking his hat off and slapping it against his leg while sighing. He didn't want to get caught up in the situation but he didn't want to see his friend get hurt either. If it'd been anyone other than Ellis he would've left him on the spot. But he couldn't turn his back on a friend who asked for his help. Especially considering he could count the amount of friends he had on one hand.

"Alright...I'm in," Symon told him.

Ellis let out a huge smile and put his arm around Symon to show his appreciation. Then the sheriff went to his desk and opened a drawer pulling out a badge for his newfound deputy. He tossed the badge to Symon who held it in his hand for a few moments gazing at it. He hesitated for a minute before putting it on still not quite sure it was a good idea.

"Looks like it was made for you," Ellis jokingly said. "How's it feel?"

"Feels like they got a better target to shoot at," Symon replied.

"Hey, what's going on out there?" Keogh shouted from his cell.

The two lawmen walked back to his cage to let him know what was happing.

"Do I see right? Is that a lawman's badge on you?" Keogh mockingly asked.

"You don't shut up I'll go away and let you fend for yourself," Symon replied.

"What do you mean?"

"Looks like the town ain't too fond of me bringing you here. There's talk of a lynching."

"I don't deserve that," Keogh yelled, pulling at the bars of his cell.

"You deserve it and more if it was possible."

"You're not gonna let them get away with that are you?" Keogh asked.

"I'm still here ain't I?"

"Thanks."

"Don't thank me. I'm not doing it for you."

"Then what are you doing it for then?"

Symon couldn't really express why he was doing it other than his friendship with Ellis. He then turned toward Ellis and nodded in his direction.

"For him," Symon explained.

"Just sit tight," Ellis told Keogh. "Nobody's gonna be lynching anybody. Unless it's over my dead body."

"Well what are the chances of that happening?!" Keogh wondered.

"Not likely."

Symon and Ellis walked back towards the window to see what was going on across the street. There was still a good amount of people gathering around talking to each other.

"Got an idea," Symon told his partner.

"What is it?"

"Follow me and let me do the talking."

The two went outside and made themselves visible to everyone just standing in front of the office. Symon was making sure that everyone could see what he now had pinned to his chest. As the crowd began looking over to the lawmen they soon realized that Symon had been deputized by the glare that emanated from the badge. Symon saw a few fingers being pointed in his direction. A few more minutes had passed and Ellis looked over at Symon and asked him a question.

"Is everything going according to plan?"

"So far."

"Mind sharing what you have in mind?"

"Don't mind a bit."

"Well go ahead."

"Just waiting."

"Waiting for what?"

"Somebody to say something," Symon said.

"About what?"

"Don't matter. Could be anything."

"I don't follow what you're thinking."

"All I need is an opening to say what I gotta say."

"Which is what?"

"You'll find out when they do," Symon said with a devilish smile.

"Can't you just walk up to them and say what you gotta say?"

"Guess I could if I had to."

"You really think someone in that bunch is gonna walk up here and challenge you?"

"Why not?"

"I think they fear your reputation," Ellis revealed.

"Well that's good."

"How long you plan on just standing here?"

"Getting tired?" Symon asked.

"Me? No. But I was just wondering."

"Alright, you win. Let's go."

Symon and Ellis broke from their stance in front of the jail and walked across the street to confront the mob of people congregating.

"Didn't you boys hear what I said before?" Ellis told the group.

"We heard you loud and clear," one man stated.

"What's going on with that other badge?" another man shouted.

"It's not your concern," Ellis replied.

"Anything that affects this town is our concern," Mendenthal retorted.

"Well then if you must know I've deputized Brice Symon till the U.S. Marshall arrives."

"He ain't no lawman," somebody said from the crowd.

Ellis started to say something before Symon took hold of his arm stopping him.

"If someone's got something to say to me then say it," Symon demanded.

The crowd fell silent as nobody was quite sure how to talk to Symon.

"Well if you all got nothing to say to me then I'll say something to you. I don't want to stay in this town any more then you want me here. I'm only here cause of you folks causing trouble. Well that's gonna stop here and now. I've got other things to do and staying here ain't one of them."

"So what is it that you're telling us, Mr. Symon?" someone asked.

"Basically it comes down to this. There ain't gonna be no trouble around that jail. There's gonna be no shootings, no stabbings, no ropes, guns, pistols, or knives. If something does happen to start around that jail then I would suggest you start making some pine boxes because I promise you that I will fill them."

"Sounds like you're threatening us."

"That I am. I make no bones about it. I'm making sure you all understand me perfectly clear. I will not tolerate any funny business," Symon continued.

"It sure sounds like he's not talking like a lawman, Paul. You gonna let someone wearing a badge talk like that and threaten to kill people?"

"Only thing I've heard him say is that he will defend his life and his prisoner. That's not illegal. That's self defense as clear as day. Surely you can see that."

"Perhaps but that doesn't change the fact that we want Keogh out of here."

"I've already told you, Mendenthal, and now I'll tell the rest of you. You're panicking over nothing. His partner's nowhere close to here and the rest of his gang is dead and buried. I can personally attest to that," Symon informed them.

"How do you know his partner's not close?" someone asked.

"Cause he wants to put as much distance between him and me as possible. Him coming here with me in the area is as foolish a thing as a man could do. And he ain't that stupid."

The crowd started to murmur as it debated within itself about what Symon had told them. They seemed to be divided about whether to still be worried or not.

"Well I'm not gonna stand here and debate with you forever," Symon told them. "I've told you how things are and how they're gonna be. I suggest you listen or suffer the consequences."

Symon and Ellis turned away from the crowd and walked back to the jail. Once inside they sat down and started talking.

"That was quite a speech you gave out there," Ellis stated.

"I wasn't figuring on it being that long-winded when I drew it up in my head."

"Well no matter that. I think it might've done the trick though."

"We'll see."

"Not convinced?"

"It only takes one idiot to stir things up. And I can't say that I haven't come across a town yet that didn't have at least one of those."

"Can't argue with you there."

Chapter 10

As the night wore on the town was eerily quiet. Ellis sensed something was not quite right as the town was usually a little more vibrant. There were usually people walking or riding along the street or he could hear all the commotion coming out of the saloon. But tonight was an uncommonly quiet night and he didn't like it. Symon had been sitting in the jail but came out to the porch of the jail where Ellis had been standing.

"Thinkin?" Symon asked.

"Yeah, I guess a little bit. Can't help it with how quiet it is out there," he responded, nodding in the town's direction.

"I was meaning to ask you about that. Is it normal to be this quiet?"

"Not a bit," Ellis answered, shaking his head.

"Well that's not a good sign."

"I know it."

"What do you think's goin' on?" Ellis wondered.

"No way of tellin' for sure."

"Think they're gonna try something?"

"Don't think they're gonna try anything right now," Symon offered.

"Why not?"

"They don't have the nerve yet. By the sound of that saloon it doesn't sound like anyone's liquored up yet. Usually takes more than a few drinks to start mustering up the courage for a lynching."

"So what do you propose we do for the rest of the night?" Ellis asked.

"Sit back, relax, try to get some sleep if you can."

"Are you crazy?"

"It's been wondered before," Symon deadpanned.

"You want me to relax with him sitting in my jail and not knowing what these idiots are planning?"

"That's the idea."

"Are you always this relaxed when you go up against someone?"

"Usually. Don't make much sense to get riled up if you can help it. Once you get mad or let your head start playing tricks on you the less good you are. Just try to give it no mind."

"Wish I had your demeanor."

"Yeah, well, I think I'm gonna head off to the hotel and try to sleep a little bit. At least one of us needs to get some sleep."

"What if something happens?"

"Just fire your gun and I'll come runnin'."

"Wouldn't it be better to stay here?"

"Nah. If they get your cornered I can sneak up from behind them and catch them by surprise."

"Seems like you got things figured out pretty good."

"Not really. Just sounds like I do," Symon said as he gave Ellis a comforting pat on the shoulder.

Symon then left to go to his room as Ellis sat in a chair in front of the jail. A few more hours passed before Ellis finally started getting groggy. He locked the door before grabbing one of the cots in the office. Another hour went by before Ellis woke up upon hearing a noise. He jumped up and grabbed his gun before looking out the window to see if he saw anything. Everything seemed as quiet as he left it though. He unlocked the door and slowly walked outside ready for anything. After looking around he decided the noise he heard was nothing and started to walk through the door before a man came up behind him and knocked him cold with a blow to the back of his head with a handgun. Ellis fell to the floor, his attacker dragging the sheriff inside and quickly closing the door eager to make sure he wasn't seen.

The man scurried over to the wall where the cell keys were kept and grabbed them. He walked over to Keogh's cell and unlocked it, the sound of the keys rattling and opening the cell waking Keogh up.

"Who are you?" Keogh asked, wondering if his time on earth was closing.

"Your new best friend."

"Huh?"

"Looks like you're being released," the man answered.

"Is this a joke?"

The man walked over to the desk and found a gun belt in one of the bottom drawers. He walked back over to Keogh and tossed the belt and a gun to him. Keogh checked to make sure it was loaded which it was.

"Much obliged to ya, friend," Keogh told the stranger.

"No problem. Mind if I ride with ya for a spell," he replied.

"What for?" Keogh asked.

"I heard your gang's been killed. Thought maybe you'd like to restart it."

"Why not?" Keogh answered with a smile.

The two men quickly left the jail and made their way to a couple of horses that were already saddled and ready to ride. As soon as the men mounted their horses Ellis had awaken and pulled his gun of the holster, firing a bullet into the floor. The shot startled the outlaws who rode hard out of town trying to get as much distance as possible in front of whoever would come after them.

Symon came running from his hotel room upon hearing the shot that Ellis had fired. He barged into the jail and noticed his friend lying on the floor, slowly getting to his knees. He then ran towards Keogh's cell and saw the door wide open with his prisoner missing. Symon went back to Ellis and helped him to his feet and then grabbed a chair for him.

"You alright?"

"Yeah, I'll be OK," Ellis slowly answered.

"What happened?"

"Don't rightly know. I was sleeping and woke up when I heard a noise. Went outside and got clobbered in the back of the head."

"Know who it was?"

"No clue."

"Well, I reckon I'll have to go after them."

"Want me to form a posse?"

"Nope, never trust 'em. They'd wind up slowing me down anyway. I'll be back in a few hours."

Symon reached inside his pocket and pulled out his deputy badge. He held it in his hand for a second, looking at it, and then tossed it on the desk.

"Reckon I won't need that where I'm goin'," he warned.

"Not likely."

Symon hurried to the stable and saddled up his horse. He brought his horse out and saw the fresh tracks of the horses racing out of town. He mounted and raced after them. He figured he could catch up to them within an hour or two.

Keogh figured Symon would be right on their trail and knew that they couldn't slow down at all. If they did they'd wind up staring down the barrel of gun he knew would fire without hesitation. He knew Symon wasn't likely to take any prisoners this time. As they were riding Keogh's new partner went down in a gulf of dust as his horse stepped in a small hole upending his rider. Keogh slowed up and turned around to see the horse galloping away without his partner on it. Keogh stopped and saw the young man staggering to his feet.

"Let me ride with you," the man said.

Keogh didn't respond as he thought about the repercussions. He looked out into the distance and he could feel Symon was coming closer. If he helped his partner he'd be slowed up considerably and there'd be no doubt that Symon would catch up to them. The man could tell that Keogh was considering leaving him there which would undoubtedly seal his fate.

"C'mon, you wouldn't even be here if it wasn't for me," he yelled out.

Keogh pondered for another second before heading towards his partner to help him on the back of his horse. Although he knew they'd be slower he figured Symon might wind up catching them anyway so he'd be better off with having an extra gunman with him.

Symon wasn't too far behind when he saw a horse riding towards him. He noticed that it was saddled and figured that he'd thrown the cowboy that rode him. After a few more minutes he slowed down a little to look at the tracks and could tell that the horse was carrying extra weight. He knew he'd run into them in minutes. Once he started riding again he could see the outline of the men he was following. As he continued on the path he noticed that the men had stopped and had turned around almost as if they were waiting for him.

"What're you doing?" Keogh was asked.

"It's useless to keep going. He's gaining on us and there ain't no way stop it."

"So what are we gonna do?"

"Well, there's two of us and one of him. Seems like the odds are in our favor."

"You mean a gunfight?"

"I'm a little tired of running. It's gonna end now one way or the other. Besides, he can't get both of us."

As Symon rode toward them he noticed them getting off the horse and he pulled up on his horse. He wondered what they were planning.

"Symon," Keogh shouted. "Is that you?"

"You know it is," Symon yelled back.

"You sure are persistent."

"Enough of the small talk, say what you gotta say."

"I figure it like this, we can't outrun ya, we both know it."

"That's a fact."

"So I figure we'll just stop right here. If you want us…come get us."

"If that's how you want it."

"That's how I want it."

"Fine with me."

Symon dismounted and started walking in the outlaws direction. They in turn started walking in his direction. After a few minutes they were within twenty feet of each other.

"Before we get started I'd like to know your friends name," Symon asked.

"Can't say I know it myself," Keogh replied.

"Well, son?" Symon asked the young looking man.

"The name is George Baxter," he informed them.

"What'd you break him out of jail for? What's he to you?"

"My chance to be famous. Make a lot of money, have a lot of women, and be known throughout the country," Baxter explained.

"Too bad you won't be any of those. You're gonna die awful young from being awful foolish."

"Mighty big talk from a guy that's outnumbered," Baxter said.

Symon noticed something moving in the grass near Baxter. He looked back to Baxter knowing he was gonna have a bigger problem any second. Symon hoped he could startle Baxter into moving unexpectedly to spur the problem on.

"If I was you son, I'd be moving," Symon warned him.

"Why's that?"

"Cause you're about to go down and it ain't gonna be from me."

"What's he talking about?" he asked Keogh.

Keogh looked a little confused, not sure what Symon was talking about, but he also wasn't gonna look and take his eyes off him.

"All you gotta do is listen," Symon told them.

The men stood silent for a few moments before hearing a small rattling sound.

"What's that?" Baxter asked.

"Sounds like a rattler that's laying right by your foot," Symon explained.

That was enough to frighten Baxter into moving unexpectedly as he jumped around to see the rattler Symon was talking about. The rattler lunged at Baxter and bit him in the stomach. Keogh tried to use the distraction to get the jump on Symon, drawing his firearm but not getting a chance to fire it as Symon cleared his holster first and lodged a couple of bullets into Keogh's chest killing him instantly. Baxter drew his pistol trying to kill the snake that still was attached to his stomach but missing with his shot. Symon realized that the kid was done for and fired a shot right through the snake which killed it and also went through Baxter's midsection causing the kid to fall to his knees. Baxter looked down and saw his stomach bleeding badly and turning a different color from the snake bite.

"I'm not gonna make it am I?" he asked Symon.

"Looks like you're done for," Symon bluntly told the youngster.

"Do me a favor and end the pain."

Symon figured it was the right thing to do to oblige the kid. He raised up his pistol one more time and fired a shot that lodged into the Baxter's forehead. Symon looked down at Baxter and shook his head at the kid's foolishness. Symon then walked over to the lifeless bodies and dragged them one at a time to their horse, flinging them over the saddle. He mounted his horse and took the reins of the other horse behind him as he began his journey back to town.

Symon arrived in town just as the sun was rising. He slowly rode to the jail with his victims following him. There wasn't much activity in town yet as most people were still sleeping or just waking up. Symon walked into the jail and saw Ellis sleeping on a cot. Symon started to make himself some coffee, and a lot of noise, hoping to wake the sheriff up. It worked as Ellis rose from his bed moments later.

"Well good morning. It's about time you woke up. Hope you slept well," Symon sarcastically said.

"Not too bad," Ellis replied, holding the back of his head.

"How you feel?"

"I've been better."

"Probably been worse too."

"Yeah, most likely. So'd you find them?"

"Wouldn't be here if I didn't."

"Where are they?"

"Out in front," Symon informed him as he took a sip of his coffee.

"Should I ask if they're alive?"

"I think you already know the answer to that."

Ellis walked outside to look at the bodies draped across one of the horses. Symon followed him out a minute later. He walked over to the horse carrying the bodies and slowly pulled them off letting them fall violently to the ground.

"They put up much of a fight?" Ellis wondered.

"Keogh had enough of running, wanted to make a final stand."

"Why that's George Baxter," Ellis said.

"Know the boy?"

"Not real well, but he hangs around town every now and then. No family that I know of. Wouldn't have figured him to do something like this."

"Looks like he wanted to get famous."

"So what are you planning to do now?" Ellis wondered.

"Finish what I started."

"Think you can find him?"

"The question ain't if…it's when. He's had a little time to put some distance between us. Man could disappear in less time than that."

"Well I wish you luck," Ellis told him as he offered his hand.

"Thank you friend," Symon replied as they shook hands.

Chapter 11

It took several months before Symon was able to pick up on Ashton's trail. He was finally able to track him to the town of Larsen City in western Colorado. By the time Symon rode through the streets of town, his horse kicking up snow, he figured he was within a day's reach of Ashton. Symon pulled up on his horse in front of the saloon and figured he'd quench his thirst and rest for a little bit. He noticed two rough looking men sitting on either side of the swinging saloon doors. They seemed to be looking at him rather intently. Symon wondered if they knew him from somewhere. He walked up to the bar and ordered a beer. As the bartender handed him his drink Symon figured he'd try for some information.

"Seen Trist Ashton around here lately?" Symon asked softly as to not allow anyone else to hear him.

"Who's askin'?"

"I am."

"He a friend of yours?" the bartender wondered.

"Nope."

"Then why are you looking for him?"

"That's my business."

"Fair enough."

"So have you seen him?" Symon asked again getting slightly annoyed.

"Depends on who you are."

"Bounty hunter."

"I thought so."

"Problem for you?"

"Nope. Don't bother me a bit," the bartender revealed.

"Well?"

"You Brice Symon?"

"Yep."

"I thought so."

"You better do less thinkin' and more talkin'," Symon stated.

"He was here this morning."

"Where did he go?"

"Not sure. He might still be in town for all I know," the bartender told him.

"Anything else?"

"I know who probably does know where he is."

"Who might that be?"

"Did you happen to see two men standing outside on your way in?"

"I recall seeing two men who seemed to be givin' me an evil eye."

"Yeah, well, it ain't cause they thought you were good looking."

"How's that?"

"Ashton sat in this very saloon this morning and hired them two fellas to kill you. I thought it was kind of ironic putting a bounty on a bounty hunter," the bartender told him as he started to laugh.

Symon took his eyes off the glass in front of him and just glared at the bartender.

"Well maybe not so ironic," the bartender quickly stated as he stopped laughing.

"So they're waiting for me, huh?"

"Yep. That's how I figured out it was you. Ashton seemed to be waiting for you."

"He knew I was close."

"You might be too close now. Them two boys are probably gonna gun you down as soon as you step out in that street," he told Symon.

"You know anything about them?"

"Not too much. They sure do look tough enough though."

"Lot of men look tough. Being tough is another question all together."

"You'd know better than I would."

"Wouldn't surprise me if Ashton was looking in on the action if something goes down out there," Symon said.

"So what do you plan on doing?" the bartender wondered.

"No idea. I'm sure they probably know that it's me that's in here."

"You can count on that."

"So how come the law isn't chasing Ashton and his goons out of here?"

"Probably would if we had any."

"You don't have a lawman here?" Symon asked in disbelief.

"Nope. Haven't had one for months. Really haven't needed one either. Not a whole lot goes on around here," the bartender explained.

Symon finished his beer and paid for his drink. He walked over to the door and took a deep breath before walking through it. He stood just outside the door and looked at the men on both sides of him.

"How you boys doin'?" Symon asked to either of them.

He didn't get a reply from either one.

"Not feelin' too hospitable today, huh?"

"We don't cotton to bounty hunters, mister," the one on the left said.

"Is that so?"

There wasn't another word said for a minute or two as the men just stood there watching the snow fall almost waiting for somebody to make a move.

"Seems to me like we got three choices here," Symon told them.

"And what are they?" the man on his right asked.

"You can tell me where Ashton is and you boys can ride out of here with no harm done."

"Don't think that's gonna happen," one of them said.

"I'll give you boys some drinkin' money while I go kill Ashton."

"Don't think that's gonna happen either."

"Well that's a darn shame for ya."

"So what's the third option?" one of them wanted to know.

"I kill the both of you where you're standing," Symon bluntly told them.

"I don't think that's gonna happen either."

"Oh no?" Symon shouted as he took off his hat throwing it in the face of the man on his left.

Symon drew his gun out of his holster as the other cowboy did the same. Symon shot him in the chest as the man fired his gun in the air while falling backwards. Symon quickly turned around within a split second as the other man had his gun drawn but it wasn't fast enough as Symon blew a hole right through his chest. It all happened within seconds. As Symon reached down to grab his hat, a shot whizzed by his head breaking the glass window of the saloon. Symon quickly jumped back into the saloon and scurried over to the window peering out. He noticed some smoke rising from the general store from across the street.

"Would that happen to be you Trist?" Symon shouted.

"It wouldn't just happen to be me, it is. The one and only."

"Looks like your plan didn't work out so well."

"Doesn't surprise me. Why do you think I was still waiting here?"

Symon and Ashton exchanged a few rounds at each other but Symon realized that nothing was gonna happen from where he was. He was gonna have to push the issue.

"Is there a back door here?" Symon asked the bartender.

"Right over there," he pointed.

"Got a shotgun I can borrow?"

The bartender nodded and handed over the shotgun behind the bar.

Symon ran out the back and went down the street using the buildings as cover for his movements. He crossed to the other side of the street hoping that Ashton didn't notice. He slipped in behind those structures through an alley. Only a few short minutes later he found himself behind the general store. Symon slowly turned the door handle careful as to not make any sounds that would alert Ashton to his presence. He proceeded to the front of the store and saw Ashton looking through the window. He raised the shotgun waiting for Ashton to turn around.

"Looking for me?" Symon asked announcing his presence.

Ashton quickly spun around with his rifle but he had no chance as Symon's shotgun put a hole right through him blowing him through the window out into the snow covered street. Symon ran out to make sure he was dead. Ashton was moving slightly and started fumbling for a gun when Symon raised the shotgun once more and fired putting an end to the outlaw's life. Symon walked over to the saloon and handed the shotgun back to the bartender.

"Much obliged to ya," Symon told him.

The bartender nodded as he took the gun back. Symon grabbed another horse to drape Ashton over before mounting his own. He took him to the nearest town to collect the money that was owed to him. After collecting his money he took out some papers from his pocket and sent them to Mary Ford that he thought she'd like.

Ford had just finished eating her lunch when someone came over to her with Symon's letter. There was no return address indicating who it was from. She opened the letter and took out the contents. It was the wanted posters of Ashton and Keogh with a big X through their faces. Half of a smile crept over her lips as she knew what that meant.

A short time later Symon had come across Baxtor Springs again passing through. He decided to pay a visit to his friend who he saw sitting in a chair in front of the jail.

"That how you make your livin' these days?" Symon shouted.

"I knew it'd been too quiet around here lately," Ellis replied.

Symon dismounted his horse and the two friends went inside the office.

"Heard you found Ashton," Ellis stated.

"Yeah."

"After someone else now?"

"Not just yet. Figured I'd relax for a little bit. Take it easy."

"Sounds like a good plan."

Symon walked over to a drawer in Ellis' desk and pulled out a stack of papers. He sorted through a few of them before picking one out of the pile.

"Thought you were taking some time off?" Ellis asked.

"Doesn't mean I can't drift in a certain direction while I am."

"Who'd you pick out?"

"Someone who's nightmare has just started."

Titles

The Assassin (Western)
Escape (Suspense/Thriller)
Day Of The Assassin (Western-short story)
Fury At Sundown (Western-short story)
Misconduct (Hockey-short story)
The Mason Files (Mystery-short story)

About the Author

Rye James was born and resides in Philadelphia, Pa with his wife, daughter, and son. He has a love of animals evidenced by his three dogs, two Labs and a Boxer. He also likes riding horses and promotes various animal charities. He's also a supporter of several children and cancer charities. You may visit Rye on the web at www.ryejamesonline.com where you can ask him questions, read his monthly interview, as well as receiving frequent updates on the latest news on his future works. He is currently working on a new novel.